Psalm 59:1 Deliver me from my enemies, O my God; protect me from those who rise up against me… (KJV)

Table of Contents

Chapter 1
Chapter 2
Chapter 3
Chapter 4
Chapter 5
Chapter 6
Chapter 7
Chapter 8
Chapter 9
Chapter 10
Chapter 11
Chapter 12
Chapter 13
Chapter 14
Chapter 15
Chapter 16
Chapter 17
Chapter 18
Chapter 19
Chapter 20
Chapter 21
Chapter 22
Chapter 23
Chapter 24
Chapter 25
Chapter 26
Chapter 27
Chapter 28
Chapter 29
Chapter 30
Chapter 31

Benen: Encouraged to Protect

The Barnabas Chronicles

Book 2

By

Ronna M. Bacon

Chapter 32
Chapter 33
Chapter 34
Chapter 35
Chapter 36
Chapter 37
Chapter 38
Chapter 39
Chapter 40
Chapter 41
Chapter 42
Chapter 43
Chapter 44
Chapter 45
Chapter 46
Chapter 47
Chapter 48
Chapter 49
Chapter 50
Epilogue
Dear Readers

Chapter 1

His hands shoved into his navy hooded sweatshirt pockets, Benen Carroll stood outside the hospital room, his gray eyes trained on the door, just waiting. Waiting for what, he wondered? The last few days, no, a week or ten days, he thought, had been a whirlwind of activity, and that not always of the good kind. He leaned his head back, his blond hair mussed, his eyes sliding closed, fatigue weighing him down. His thoughts drifted as the sounds of the activity normally found on a hospital floor faded around him.

He thought back to two weeks ago, when a letter had arrived, a letter from people in his past, people he no longer saw, but had been a frequent guest in their home in the past. The couple, now serving as missionaries in a Latin America country, had asked for his help. He could not refuse. They had become family, almost, to him when his mother had passed away from cancer when he was twenty. He didn't remember his father, losing his father when he was so young, to cancer as well.

He had read the letter and then set it aside, knowing he needed to pray over it. What they asked would change his life, that much he knew. He had finally gone to his friend and boss, Barnabas Carey, who ran The Barnabas Foundation, an foundation that provided help to those in need. Benen worked as an IT specialist but his wages were paid for by the Foundation. He had asked for two weeks off, to

—

travel to see the family. Barnabas had shot him a long look, scrutinized his face for a few minutes, and then nodded, asking that he call if he needed any help. Benen had nodded, knowing he would not do that.

He had taken a private flight down, the airplane part of the Foundation arsenal of transportation, and landed, heading for the mission where he knew he would find his friends. He had not expected to land in a country torn apart by riots and war. He had feared for their lives, knowing that they would be targets.

After clearing customs, he had shouldered his backpack and headed away from the airport, knowing Andy would fly home and then return in about seven days. He wended his way through the crowds, mobs almost, he thought, noting the high presence of police and military personnel. He shook his head as he was jostled roughly. What had he walked into and just what did it mean for his friends? His eyes constantly searched the crowds, feeling himself being watched but he could not find who it was.

The couple, Mary and Ted Daniell, had greeted him, welcomed him into their home. They had been there for years, and were scheduled to leave for their furlough back at home. Only this time, they wouldn't be coming back. That much they knew. Their mission board had deemed it too dangerous and were pulling their people out.

The day before he was to fly home, Ted approached Benen with a request. Benen had stared at him and then at Mary, his eyes then moving to their daughter, Cadee, who was his age and had been a good friend of his in college. He watched the emotions flickering across her face before he agreed. Even as he did so, he was not sure he was doing right, but God had not spoken to stop him. And Benen had enough faith to know that God would step in.

The parents had fled very early the next morning, heading for another country and safety and then a flight home to Ontario, Canada, where they had a home on the shores of Lake Erie. Cadee, they knew, would be safe with Benen.

Benen had stared at the door as it closed behind them, then turned to Cadee.

"Cadee?" He ran his hand through his thick blond hair, his intense dark blue eyes troubled.

She had turned, her dark brown eyes hiding her emotions, her own dark blond hair, cut to shoulder length, swinging around her face as she did so. "Benen? Now what?"

"Now what is that we grab what we can stuff into our backpacks and then head for the airport. Andy said he'd be there by this morning." He stood for a moment, not sure if she would even come with him, feeling his jacket pocket for the envelope of paperwork he had been handed by Ted.

She nodded, her steps rapid as she moved to pack what she could, handing him his own pack. She looked around, sorrow briefly showing on her face. "Let's go. We'll need to walk. It's a hike, you know."

"I know." He reached for her hand, stopping her movements. "First, we need to pray. We're not going to make it unless God goes ahead of us."

Their movements hampered by the crowds milling in the streets, they walked away from the mission and headed for the airport, Cadee's hand tight in his. Jostled, almost torn away from one another, they forged ahead, Benen's eyes watchful. He heard a whimper from Cadee at one point and turned, finding her rubbing at her shoulder.

"Cadee? What happened?"

"I felt a sting. Likely a bug of some kind." She pulled him with her. "There's the airport. We made it."

He glanced down at the watch on his left wrist and nodded. "We did. Just in time." After clearing customs, which didn't take long to his surprise, he rushed her towards the airplane and up the stairs into it, nodding at the pilot, before he pointed to a seat.

"Sit there, Cadee. Buckle up. Andy's ready to take off as soon as we're situated." He tucked their packs away, then chose a seat near her, nodding to Andy's question of were they ready as he did so. He felt the plane lift off, the start of a long flight, he knew.

Towards the end of the flight, he had turned to Cadee, concerned. He watched as she slept, her head against a pillow he had tucked behind it, wrapped in the soft yellow blanket he had found. He was concerned, that was a given. He moved to touch her, dismayed at the clamminess of her skin, the dark shadows that were appearing under her eyes, her paleness, the occasional spike of a fever he had felt over the last couple of hours.

—

He moved forward to stand in the cockpit doorway.

"How long, Andy?" He squinted through the darkening skies, knowing it was getting to the early evening on that winter day.

"Just coming up to start the descent. Making it through customs a bit ago was a breeze, for some reason. I've never seen it go so fast." He studied his instruments before him, then glanced at the runway lights as he prepared for their approach. "Buckle up, Benen." He shot a quick glance at Benen. "How's your lady?"

"She's not well. I don't know why. She was fine earlier this morning." He returned to his seat, his eyes on Cadee.

He carried her to his car, his thanks ringing in Andy's ears as the pilot placed their luggage in the car trunk, and then stood back, watching before he slammed the door and ran for his seat, speeding away, instinct telling him that he needed to get to the hospital and fast. Something was wrong with her and she needed medical attention.

He roused as the nurse touched his arm, pointing to the door, before he nodded, his footsteps heavy as he moved that way, coming to stand at the end of the bed, watching Cadee, wishing he knew what the problem was.

He finally pulled a chair close to the bed, and sat, his elbows on his knees, hands clasped, chin resting on his thumbs, his eyes not moving from Cadee as she lay, motionless. He studied the heart monitor, the IV pole and its bags of IV fluid and antibiotics, heard the slight hiss of the oxygen from the nasal prongs as she struggled to breathe. He didn't look around as he heard the door swish open and footsteps approach.

"Benen?" Barnabas spoke, his eyes on his friend, a frown in place. "What's going on? Andy said you were back but that you headed right here with the lady you brought back with you."

Benen didn't move, simply shifted his eyes to stare at Barnabas before they shifted to the man with him, Branigan Clery, his own team leader. He sighed, knowing that when he spoke, things would be changed. Lord, he thought, I had no idea this was in the works when I agreed to help the Daniells. I really didn't, but You did.

"Benen?" This time, it was Branigan who spoke, his eyes full of concern, before he turned as the door opened and a physician entered.

Benen was on his feet, swaying slightly from fatigue, watching closely as the physician assessed Cadee and then motioned for the nurse to hang another bag to the IV pole.

"Doc?" Benen's voice was quiet, hopeful, yet with a tone to it that said he accepted the inevitable. By this time, it was early morning and he had been anxiously awaiting the results of the testing.

"Benen, we ran the blood work we spoke of. You were correct. What she thought was a bug bite wasn't." The physician gently moved the hospital gown closer to her neck, exposing the area on her shoulder that showed a red, almost angry looking mark. "She was poisoned. It looks as if she moved the dart or whatever it was before she took in too much, but there was enough to cause this. Who does she have for enemies?"

Benen shrugged, his mind sorting through what little Ted had been able to tell him.

"Considering where we just came back from, who knows, Doc." He spoke with the physician for a few more moments, and watched as he walked away.

"Benen? Care to explain? I know where Andy took you and brought you back from." Barnabas watched Benen, a frown on his face. "Who is she?"

"Cadee?" Benen's hand traced down her hair, stopping to rest on her cheek. "She's an old friend, Barnabas." He paused, swallowing hard, his eyes still on Cadee, wishing she would awaken and help him say what he needed to say. He finally spoke once more. "And my wife."

—

Chapter 2

When he uttered those words, Benen had no idea of the effect they would have on his friends, or the relief that he felt when he acknowledged it. He knew, he thought, that he would have to tell them, but just not like this. Not with Cadee laying there, not knowing if she would live or die. His heart raised in prayer for her, for her parents, for the ones they had had to leave behind in the war-torn country.

"Benen? What on earth are you talking about? You're not married! You're not even dating anyone."

Barnabas' voice broke through his thoughts. He heard the questions, the concern, in it. He finally looked around, seeing Barnabas and Branigan exchanging looks.

"Barnabas? It's too long a story for now." He sank back into his chair, fatigue washing through him, a bleak look around his eyes. "Can we talk tomorrow? Or rather later today?" He amended this question as he glanced at his watch, seeing it was early morning by then.

"Benen?" Branigan's voice came from beside him, Branigan's hand on his shoulder. "We have no idea what you're facing or what's going on. Let us pray for you."

Benen nodded, his eyes not leaving Cadee's face. "Listen, guys. Can you tell the others before I bring her home? If I even get to do that." He blinked at the moisture blocking his vision. "You heard the physician. She was poisoned as we were almost to the plane. We still don't know why or who."

"Benen? What did you go and get involved in?" Barnabas' voice held concern, but also a touch of frustration and worry.

"You know the country we came from. Her parents were missionaries there. Cadee had been visiting them for a few months, working in the office for them. I didn't know when they asked me for help just what all was at stake. They couldn't put it into writing. It was too dangerous for them, for Cadee, and for myself, if I chose to go there." Benen turned slightly to watch his friends. "The Daniells themselves slipped away to another country to escape and make their way back here. That's how afraid they are for all of them. I had to bring Cadee back. The only way to do that safely was for her to have a name change. That's what they asked of me, yesterday. They asked if I would give her the protection of my name and then bring her back with me. The minister from their church married us."

Barnabas approached him, standing with his hand on Benen's shoulder as he prayed.

"Now, is there a chance they have followed you?"

Benen shrugged. "I guess. Andy wasn't on the ground too long." He looked down at Cadee for a moment, watching her restless movements. "The thing of it is, Barnabas? There is a contract out on her. She saw something, someone, knows something, has something that she shouldn't have. We just don't know what."

—

"And you're afraid they'll follow you to here?" Branigan spoke up.

"I am. We don't know who, so we can't be prepared." Benen watched Cadee as she moved more restlessly, her mouth working as she tried to swallow, her tongue flicking out between her lips as she tried to moisten them. He reached to cradle her head in one hand as with the other he carefully fed her ice chips, the only thing the physician would allow her.

Barnabas and Branigan moved away, their eyes on the young couple, as they spoke quietly, before Barnabas walked away, leaving Branigan leaning against the wall outside the room, his eyes on Benen. He finally shook his head. First Baird, marrying Berneen like he did, saving his life. Branigan gave a small smile. That couple was working out just fine, he thought, deeply in love despite what they had been through. He tilted his head to study Benen, a frown on his face. Something else was going on there, he thought. Then he sighed. They're more than old friend, aren't they, Lord, at least on his part.

Benen finally sat back down, his eyes on Cadee, willing her to awake, but knowing that she couldn't, not just yet. He had been warned that it may take days. He twisted in his chair, trying to find a comfortable position, pulling the blanket tight around him, his eyes finally sliding closed as he slept, exhausted from the trip, the worry, and his fear for Cadee.

Branigan watched before he turned as he heard his name called gently. Doc Whitson stood there, a frown on his face.

—

"Branigan?"

"Benen's here, Doc." He looked towards the partly open door. "He's in there."

Doc stepped to the door. "That's why I'm here. Tom called me in. He wants me up to speed on her for when she goes home."

"She will be going home, Doc? Benen doesn't seem to believe that."

"She will be. Thanks to Benen's question, she will be. Tom said I need to be aware of what's going on with her." Doc looked around before he handed Branigan the cup of coffee he was carrying for him. "What's this I hear though? Benen's wife?"

"Apparently so. It's quite the story, though." He looked around as he heard footsteps approaching and a nurse entered Cadee's room. He frowned and then shrugged. What did he know about schedules in the hospital?

Chapter 3

Her eyes flickering open and closed, Cadee finally roused, her hand searching for her aching head, the very touch on it sending the pain wafting through it stronger. She squeezed her eyes shut, wondering just what she had gone and done that she didn't remember going and doing. She tried to moisten her dry mouth and lips and couldn't.

She felt a gentle hand raising her head, the touch soft and careful. A glass touched her lips and she swallowed, greedy to drink, protesting with a whimper when the glass was moved back before she had had enough of the water.

"It's okay, Cadee. You can have more." A voice, familiar, from her past she thought, spoke but before she could respond, she drifted back to sleep.

Doc stood and watched for a moment before he looked at Benen. "That's a natural sleep, Benen. Given what she's been through, I would not have expected it yet."

"She has always healed quickly from whatever she's had." Benen stood, an arm leaning on the side rail of the bed, the other hand gently moving her hair back from her face.

Doc nodded, then spoke. "We'll get her home likely by tomorrow, if all goes well."

"Plan for this afternoon, Doc. I know her. She'll walk out of here today if she can."

Doc shook his head, before he laughed. "I'll have Anna go through your place, tidying it up for you. Any special instruction?"

Benen hesitated, then nodded. "The yellow room? The spare room? Can you put some yellow roses in there for her?" He didn't see the look Doc gave him, his attention back on Cadee as she moved.

He didn't hear Doc walk away, didn't hear the footsteps that approached quietly and then turned and walked away. His sole focus was Cadee.

Cadee roused once more, feeling a hand touching her face gently and a voice talking to her, asking her to awaken. She turned into the hand, thinking it was familiar, but not sure.

"Cadee? Come on, darling. Time to rise and shine. Wake up, sleeping beauty."

Cadee cracked an eye open, then closed it, the light bright for a moment. She blinked, trying to clear her vision before her eyes opened once more and stayed open. She glanced around, searching for what she didn't know, before her eyes landed on the man standing by her bedside, his head tilted to see her face, a smile on his.

"Benen Carroll?" She swallowed from the glass he held to her mouth. "What are you doing here?"

He shook his head. "You don't remember?"

She shook her own. "No, I don't." She looked around the room once more. "Where am I?"

"In the hospital back in Ontario. You've been sick." He hesitated to tell her exactly what had happened.

"Sick? By the way I feel, it's much more than just that." She stared at him before he nodded.

"It is, Cadee. You were poisoned over twenty-four hours ago. We didn't know until you won't wake up when we landed and I got you to treatment here."

"What is going on, Benen?" She shifted in the bed, trying to sit up, nodding when he raised the head of the bed. "There's more to that than what you have said."

He sighed, knowing he would have to tell her, holding out the glass, this time her hands reaching for it, his cupping hers gently.

She stared at his hand, catching the light reflecting off his wedding band. "Benen! You're married! When? Where's your wife? You shouldn't be here with me!" She was growing agitated before her hand raised and she stared at her own finger, seeing a wedding band on it. "This can't be happening. I'm not married. I'm not even dating!" She searched the room again. "Mom? Dad? Where are they? Are they safe?"

"I'm not sure where they are at this moment, Cadee. They crossed the border to make their way back here. They were recalled by the mission."

"We were? I don't remember?"

"What is the last date you remember?"

She thought, giving him a date, the day before he arrived in the country.

"I landed there the next day. Your parents wrote to me, asking me to come." He paused, sorrow in his heart as he realized she had forgotten him being there. "You don't remember?"

She shook her head, her eyes wide as she watched him. "No. Should I?"

He reached for her left hand, laying the palm of his left hand along the top of hers, his fingers curling between hers, their rings side by side, his face thoughtful, not quite sure how to say what he needed to say.

"Benen? What are you doing?" She tugged at her hand but he refused to release it.

"You have no memory of your dad writing to me, asking me to come?"

She shook her head again. "No, they didn't tell me that they had. It's been so many years."

"It has been." He bit at his upper lip, pulling it down, his eyes on their hands. "They wrote me for a specific reason, not telling me until the day before we left to come back here. They told me you were in a danger, that they had had word a contract was put out on you for what reason, we don't know. They feared for your very life." His eyes lifted to her, a look in them she could not read. "They felt they knew me well enough to ask something of me, something that would keep you alive and get you back here."

"Benen?" Her head began to shake and he felt her hand trembling under his. The dark shadows had deepened under her eyes, the shadow of pain and something else in them. "What did they ask of you?"

"They asked me to bring you home while they made their own way back. There was a catch. They were told the only way to get you out safely was by a private plane but there was something else. Someone would be watching for you flying out under your name." He paused again, once more biting at his lip, as his eyes traced her familiar face, seeing the changes the last few years had brought and seeing also the fear she was living under.

"What did you do?"

"Your father asked if I would marry you, giving you the protection of my name and myself. He knows the organization I work for. He has spoken many times with Barnabas, without your knowledge of that."

"We did what?" Her voice rose to a squeak even as her head shook. "Tell me we didn't."

"I'm sorry, Cadee. I can't tell you that. We discussed it and both agreed it was the only way. You did say you would marry me. The minister from your church performed the ceremony. We fled the next day. We spent the time between our wedding and early the next morning packing up, making arrangements for your things to be shipped back to here, your father making sure the people there would be all right."

She was shaking her head. "We didn't. We couldn't have." She watched as his head nodded. "Benen? Tell me we didn't."

"I'm sorry, Cadee. We are married. You are my wife." He released her hand and walked away, out of the room, knowing her well enough to know she needed some time on her own, to absorb what he had just said, given that she didn't remember it.

Cadee watched him walk away, her hand to her mouth, even as her mind tried to take in what he had said. Exhaustion overcame her will to think it through, and she slept.

Chapter 4

Cadee pulled the blanket up tighter around her neck, not used to the colder weather now, she thought. She had protested when Benen had wrapped it around her, saying she didn't need it. It was the next day after the earthshaking news that they were now married, husband and wife, and that she just couldn't comprehend. They had been good friends at college and then drifted apart once they graduated.

She turned her head to stare at Benen, finding him with his face turned towards the window of the vehicle, not watching her. She sighed to herself. How did they do this, she wondered?

Benen knew Cadee was uncomfortable with him and that he regretted. He prayed for her memory to return, but the physicians hadn't been too sure on that. He had heard her protests when he had wrapped her in the blanket, positioned her in the wheelchair and headed down to the lobby doors where Branigan waited. She had protested when he had gathered her into his arms and placed her in the backseat of his car, Branigan at the wheel, before he walked slowly around, his eyes on her the whole time, to take a seat beside her, making sure she was buckled into her seatbelt.

They needed to talk, he thought, not just about them. They needed to find out who was after her and why. Right now, he didn't think she knew, but if she did, she might well have hidden it deep into her mind.

She did that with unpleasant things, he remembered only too well.

He didn't see his friends in the truck ahead of them or the SUV behind them as they pulled away. Branigan and Barnabas had called a meeting early that morning, explaining to the men about Benen and Cadee, bringing surprise and shock to most of their faces, acceptance on Baird Cassidy's face. Baird and his wife, Berneen, had been married not long before this, Berneen agreeing to it to save Baird's life. They only had one question: What could they do to help Benen?

Benen stood for a moment, his eyes on the building that housed not only their own offices, but their homes as well, staring at it, realizing he had no idea how changed his life would be when he returned, that he would not be coming home just by himself. He sighed, not seeing Barnabas standing in the lobby, his own eyes on Benen.

Benen once more gathered Cadee into his arms, walking towards through the lobby, his eyes on her face for a moment, ignoring her protests.

"Benen! I can walk!" She waited for a moment. "Put me down!"

Benen leaned back in the elevator, a nod to Barnabas as he stepped in, pushing the button for the third floor. He waited until the doors closed and then spoke.

"Cadee, you are not strong enough to walk. If we didn't have a physician on site, you would not have been allowed out yet. The physicians recommended against it."

"I wasn't that sick. I would know if I had been." She coughed, trying to hide it.

Benen's mouth tightened in frustration and almost anger. "Cadee, this is not the time or place for this conversation. Suffice it to say, a day and a half ago, they had no idea what was wrong with you. You were getting sicker and sicker. They had prepared me, you know, that you would not recover. That this was it for you." He stared down at her for a moment, seeing the shock on her face. "That's right. You were that close. God worked in your life, healing you enough that you could come home. The physician told me that if you had received just a tiny bit more of the poison, you would not have made it to the plane."

She grew quiet, her eyes huge, her mind trying to absorb what he had said. She didn't see the look of compassion on Barnabas' face as he listened to the two.

Barnabas unlocked and then opened the door for Benen, stepping in after him, setting the keys on the countertop in the kitchen before he reached for the coffee pot. He knew Benen would want something. Just what Cadee liked, he had no idea.

Benen set Cadee down on the double bed in his spare room and then knelt to remove her shoes, rising to set them tidily in the cupboard. He reached into the dresser, pulling out her night clothes, silently thanking whoever of the men had brought their luggage. He knew it was likely Anna who had unpacked for Cadee.

"Do you want a shower, Cadee? Something to drink? Or just to change and climb into bed?"

She stared at him, not sure what to think, or even what she wanted to do. "A shower would be nice, but I'm really not sure if I can manage."

He nodded, then turned to walk away. "I'll be right back."

He paused as he saw Barnabas. "Thank, Barnabas, for all you've done."

Barnabas shrugged. "It's what we do for each other. Is she settled?"

"No. Do you know if Berneen is home?"

"She should be. She told me last night she'd be around today, at least for a while." He watched as Benen headed for the door and the apartment next door.

Benen tapped at the door of Baird's apartment, not sure if he should be even doing that. He stepped back, turning to walk away, when the door flew open and Berneen stood there.

"Benen! You're home. Welcome home." She reached to hug her friend before stepping back.

"Berneen! Good to see you." Benen began to smile. "Does Baird know you're wearing his favourite T-shirt?" Berneen had on Baird's T-shirt with the logo of his favourite sports team.

Berneen smirked. "No, he doesn't. It will be back in his drawer before he's home."

Benen began to laugh as he saw Baird appear behind Berneen. "Sure about that?"

"I am!" She gave a squeal as arms came around her and Baird dropped a kiss on her cheek.

"Now I know what you're up to when I'm not home." He reached to shake Benen's hand. "Benen? How are you? Really."

Benen shrugged. "Struggling. Doubting. Knowing I need to protect her but not sure how or from whom."

Baird nodded, knowing somewhat how he felt. "Katie?"

"I'm sorry?"

"Katie? Isn't that her name?" Baird was puzzled, not sure why Benen had questioned him.

"No, it's Cadee. C-a-d-e-e. Unusual, I know. I have a favour to ask, Berneen. Say no if you have to."

Berneen took one look at him and then nodded. "She needs help, doesn't she?"

Benen sighed, grateful that he didn't have to put it into words and beg. "She does. Thank you, Berneen."

She was away and in his apartment before he was finished, leaving Benen staring after her.

"Benen, now that we're alone, how are you really? I know what you said, but there's more."

Benen leaned against the door, a hand drawn down his face, praying that he could put into words how he felt. "She doesn't remember, Baird. She doesn't remember me arriving there."

Baird's face tightened and his heart felt for his friend. "She doesn't remember marrying you, is that what you're saying?"

Benen nodded. "It is. The physician I talked to said that can sometimes happen. Trauma drives recent events away from the mind. She may or may not remember. He couldn't tell me that." Benen turned. "Thanks for praying, Baird."

"It's a given, Benen. You know that." Baird walked beside Benen back to his apartment and then stood in the kitchen, his head shaking at Barnabas. He could hear quiet words down the hall before Benen's footsteps were heard returning to the kitchen.

Chapter 5

Late that afternoon, Benen looked up from his computer where he had been trying to sort out a complex problem for a client and then saved what he was working on before he arose and walked out into the hallway, intent on finding Cadee. He found her right outside the office door, a frightened look on her face that didn't disappear when she saw him.

"Cadee?" He stooped to peer into her face, his hands on her upper arms.

"Where are they, Benen?"

"Where are who?" He really wasn't sure what she was meaning, but fear began to grow within him. He knew then, without a shadow of a doubt, that she was aware of what had been threatened.

"Them. Whoever they are that are after me. They won't let me go. They'll follow you here." She blinked back sudden tears, something he knew she regretted and didn't want him to see.

"The ones after you? I don't know, darling. You know who they are, don't you?" He swept her into a tight hug as she nodded. "Can you tell me about it?"

She shook her head. "I can't, Benen. I don't know enough about them or why they're after me to know what to say."

He turned her towards the living room, one arm around her, and made her sit on the couch, walking to the kitchen and back with a bottle of water for her.

"Here, drink this first. Then you can tell me what you want to drink. Anna left soup for you. She was by last night with it."

"Who's Anna?" She was puzzled, knowing there were people in his life she didn't know and for some reason that scared her.

"Anna is Doc's wife. She mothers us all." Benen sat beside her, his back against the couch arm, watching her. "Tell me what you can, Cadee. We'll research it. I know my friends. They won't stop until they solve it."

She looked horrified and terrified at the same time. "They can't. They'll be hurt." She watched him shake his head. "They will be."

"They know that. Some day, ask Berneen to tell you their story. It's not one I would believe if I hadn't been involved." He paused, watching her, knowing he would have to explain. "It's like this. Berneen had been abducted and held. Baird was abducted. We went in and got them out. They were abducted again the next day or so along with Buckley, who is a minister. He was forced to marry them to save Baird's life. It all came down to revenge against them for something that had happened in the past with their fathers."

She looked shocked. "What? You would never know it. Berneen is so much in love with him."

"And he with her. God worked it out. If Berneen had asked for her freedom, Baird would have given it to her, but he would never ever have married again.”

“That’s sad, you know.” She leaned her head back on the couch, shifting so she faced him. “Is that what will happen with us? We’ll go our separate ways?”

“I don’t know, Cadee. God brought us together. He could have stopped the wedding, but He didn’t. We prayed about it and agreed that we should go ahead. If one of us had had any doubts, we would not have. You know how your parents are.”

She nodded, a yawn catching her by surprise. “We do need to talk, Benen. I just don’t think today’s the day.”

“It’s not.” He grinned at her, impishness in his eyes. “Do you want something to eat?”

“That sounds good. Did you say soup?”

“I did. If I know Anna, it’s likely her homemade chicken soup. It’s so delicious.” He rose, his hand extended for her to grasp.

She studied his hand for a moment, studied the wedding band she could see, and then took his hand, reaching out in faith, knowing from past experience with him she had nothing to fear from him but that he would do his best to protect her.

Chapter 6

Two days later, Cadee slumped into a chair in Benen's office, not saying a word, watching him hard at work, recognizing in his posture the friend from years previous when he was determined to solve a problem. She wished he would solve hers, and then they could get on with their lives. Would it be with him, she wondered? She had tried hard to hide the crush she had had on him during college, not sure if he returned her feelings or not, and if he had, he had not shown it.

Benen had glanced up with a smile and asked how she was before his attention was back on the problem. She could hear his side of the conversation and realized he had changed what his planned occupation had to have been. He had been determined to teach, but now it looked as if he worked with computers. She shook her head. She wasn't the only one who had changed then, she decided.

Benen finally sat back, rubbing at his neck, rotating his shoulders and neck to relieve the stress. This problem had been a long one to solve, with the computers of a small company, but he was confident he had managed to do just that. He had no desire to fly across the country to work on them.

He looked up to find Cadee's eyes on him, a frown in place, as she curled up in a chair, unknowing taking the one he favoured, the afghan he kept there wrapped around her.

"I'm sorry, Cadee. How long?"

"How long? What do you mean?" Her voice was low, and he could hear the fatigue in it.

"How long were you here? I tend to get lost when I'm working." He rose to move beside her, crouching down and resting an arm on the chair.

"You always did. No one could get your attention if you were problem solving." She watched him closely, seeing the changes life had made in him. "Were you finished?"

"I am." He watched her closely. "You're about to ask me something."

"Stop doing that." She shoved at him with her socked foot, causing him to grab for the chair arm as he laughed. "I was. I need to find work. If I can't go back to the mission down there, I need to find something to do. There's no point in going back to the office in the headquarters here. There's no place for me."

Benen nodded, then rose, reaching for her hand. "Up for a bit of a walk? We need to go talk to Barnabas."

She slid her feet into her slippers and then looked down. "I'm not dressed to meet someone that rich."

Benen began to laugh, drawing a cross look from her. "Darling, it doesn't matter. Barnabas doesn't flaunt his wealth. If you were to meet him on the street, you would never know."

"I highly doubt that." She walked with him, her hand in his, waiting for the elevator, before she spoke again. "You did say he pays your wages?"

"He does, darling. He pays them, so that frees up a company to hire someone else if they need to, without having to worry about finding the money to do so. We all also volunteer in various capacities in different organizations. You met Baird. He volunteers as a tutor. Berneen is still trying to decide if she wants to work or just volunteer."

"What is your volunteer work, Benen? I should know."

"That you should. I had been going to the nearby prison and teach computer basics, helping to train the prisoners to find work when they're released"

She stared at him. "You never used to want to go anywhere near a jail. What happened?"

"God. And then Barnabas. He encouraged me to do that, telling me that I had nothing to fear. That God was my Protector and He walk in there with me." He held the door open so she could exit, watching in amusement as her mouth dropped and then snapped close. "I no longer do that, volunteering in a camera club instead."

She turned slowly in a circle, her hand pulling Benen with her. "This can't be real. It's like something out of a movie."

"It's real. Barnabas and his father spent a lot of time designing this, choosing the materials very carefully." He tapped his foot on the floor. "Real hardwood floors. The tiling, the walls, the seating arrangements at either end, the fireplaces?" When she nodded, he continued. "They are not that expensive, not really. He put this in to welcome clients that we have come through, but more importantly, he wanted this building to be home to each of us. He lives here himself. His parents used to until his dad retired. He wanted something warm and welcoming for us."

"I would say he succeeded." She frowned as she spied the security desk. "But you have security."

"We need to. Barnabas is very wealthy in his own right but The Barnabas Foundation could be a target. It's not common knowledge what he does with that. Security is there as a protection for us all. We don't always have the best of clients come through."

She shook her head. "And here I thought I left danger behind."

"No, unfortunately, you didn't. We still need to talk about that, though." He opened the door to The Foundation Office, grinning at Barnabas' secretary. "Amy, this is Cadee."

Cadee stared at her. "I thought you were Anna."

"She's my younger sister. They say we do look alike." Amy reached to hug Cadee, surprising her before she hugged Benen. "Welcome to the Foundation family, Cadee. Benen, Barnabas is free. He's been expecting you this afternoon." She threw up her hands as Cadee stared at her. "I have no idea how he knows these things. He can't explain it himself, other than to say God."

—

Barnabas appeared in his office doorway, leaning against the doorframe as he watched Benen and Cadee speaking with Amy. He shook his head. *What is it with these guys of mine? These two, anyway. Both of them married, and I would say that these two in front of me love each other but are afraid to say anything. Lord, protect them. Bring them through the fire I just know they are going to face.*

Benen looked up at that point, a grin on his face at the teasing Amy had been sending his way.

"Barnabas? You're free?"

"That I am. Come on in and bring your lovely bride with you."

Cadee started at Barnabas, not quite sure if he was serious or not, before her eyes lifted to Benen, who was smiling down at her.

"He means it, Cadee. I can see the question in your eyes." Benen seated her on the soft leather sofa before he headed for the kitchenette off the office, returning with the spiced apple tea she seemed to like and a coffee for himself and Barnabas, who had sat in a deep leather chair facing the couch, having dropped a folder on the table between them.

Barnabas gave a quiet thanks, watching as Benen slid to a seat beside Cadee and reached for her hand. "Welcome, Cadee. I don't think you remember me speaking with you in the hospital."

She shook her head. "Not really. Did you?"

Barnabas grinned at her. "I did. You weren't very clear on your answers though."

She groaned. "Please tell me I didn't answer stupidly."

"No, you didn't. You just couldn't answer some things, told me to ask you later." He sipped at his coffee before setting it on the table beside his chair. "We need to talk about what you're going through. The guys are all wanting to help, to free you from the fear and yes terror you're under. Don't deny it. We know that's what's been going on." He nodded at Benen. "Benen has been able to tell us what your father has told him. We need to talk to you."

She sighed. "I know you do, but Dad knew everything I did. I have no idea who or why. I don't remember seeing something or someone I shouldn't have."

"Let it rest. You'll remember, likely at the worst time possible. We will want you to go through your things when they arrive, see if there's something that doesn't belong to you." He looked at Benen for a moment. "Benen tells me that your father asked that your belongings be shipped here. That is not a problem."

"He did?" She turned to study Benen, finding him nodding at her. "I wonder why."

"Because this is your home, Cadee, darling. At least for now." Benen looked over at Barnabas. "We need to explain something to you, Cadee, and I fear you will have the same reaction as Berneen."

—

Chapter 7

Barnabas began to laugh at that, drawing Cadee's shocked look to him. "She did protest, very vehemently, if I recall." He reached for the folder, handing it to her, hesitation on her part to take it. "Benen has explained about the Foundation and how the men are paid?"

She nodded. "He did. I don't understand how it affects me."

Barnabas nodded. "Berneen was the same. It is written into our charter that when the men marry, their wives will receive a salary from the Foundation as well. That frees them to either stay at home, work out in the community, or volunteer."

She stared at him, her mouth open until she felt Benen's finger tapping her chin. She shut it was a click, a dumbfounded look on her face. "Are you for real?" At his nod, she slumped back on the couch, her eyes shifting between the two men. "For real?" Benen nodded this time. "I don't believe this." Her eyes filled with tears. "Do you know what this means to me? I can do so much now that I couldn't before."

Benen's arm around her, he hugged her to him. "That's what it was set up for, darling. For you to use as you want. If you have plans you want to put in place, talk to Barnabas. There is funding available."

She stared at him, a hand reaching to swipe at the tears on her face. "Benen, do you know how many women and children I can help? Help them to assimilate into life here? Learn about God?"

Barnabas blinked back tears himself. He had not expected that reaction, not after Berneen being adamant that she didn't want him to pay her. They had finally agreed that he would, but she was still reluctant to take the money.

"Cadee, when you're ready, come talk to me. This is what the Foundation does - what you want to do. We'll work it out." He paused, his eyes on the floor for a moment, before he looked up. "Now, I have word your belongings will be here next week. For now, do what Doc has suggested. Rest. Eat well. Sleep when you need to. You were through a trauma in more ways than one." He looked at Benen, finding him watching his bride. "You and Benen need to talk at some point. But for now, we'll focus on what happened to you and why and who is responsible. Anything you can tell us, anything that you don't think is important, let us know."

She nodded, a shadow crossing her face, leaving paleness in its wake. "I will. It's just so hard to concentrate and think right now."

Barnabas nodded once more. "We get that, Cadee. We really do. All the fellows have approached me, Benen, offering to help in any way they can."

"I've talked to my team and I know the other team is the same." He rose, drawing Cadee to her feet and then scooping her into his arms, his eyes on her face as her eyes slid closed. "We'll talk, Barnabas. Soon."

"Let's. The men want to meet in the morning. Does that work?"

Benen thought through his work outlined for the morning. "It should. If it doesn't, I'll let you know."

—

40

"And Anna said she'll be up to stay with Cadee."

Chapter 8

Dropping his portfolio on the table in the conference room, Benen headed for the coffee and poured a mug, turning to return to his seat, finding Buckley Cullen, the minister in the group, standing in front of him, his hand extended.

"Congratulations, Benen. I hope to meet your bride soon."

"You do need to do that." Benen ran his hand through his hair, deep in thought. "You all do. I just don't know though."

"She's recovering?"

"She is, but stress can tire her." Benen turned as Branigan spoke from beside him.

"We'll do a meal on the weekend, Benen. One of our potlucks. We're due for that. You two come, introduce her to us, and then we eat. You can leave at any time." He reached for his own mug of coffee. "No pressure. We want to do what we can to alleviate that for you, and to solve the mystery. None of us want to see you two go through the horror that Baird and Berneen did."

"No, we don't want that. Not for any of us." Benen slid his chair closer to the table, arranging his mug on the table to his liking and then looked towards the middle of the table where Barnabas had seated himself. "Barnabas? We're ready to start?"

"We are. First, though, prayer. What requests to we have? Benen?"

The men shared their requests and then broke into groups of two to pray, finishing as Barnabas pulled his Bible towards him.

"I have felt led to study protection in the last few days. God is our Protector. The Psalms are filled with cries for protection and praise for it. Benen, you and Cadee have been on my mind today. I fear for you two. May God hide you in the hollow of the rock and cover you both with His hand." He looked around the table. "Now, where do we stand?"

Brody Corcoran, the paralegal in the group, stood, passing around a folder to each man. "This is what I have found out about the mission the Daniells were with. It's not on the up and up. It seems to have been sabotaged somehow in the last month. Were you aware of that, Barnabas?"

"I was. I have sent in a team to work with the mission. We are trying to contact the Daniells but have had no luck as yet. Benen?"

"I haven't heard from them, and I know Cadee hasn't. They were to be here tomorrow. If they're not, they agreed to send me a text and let me know where they are. I told them we'd go in and get them."

"That's correct. Any way to contact them before then?"

Benen shook his head. "Ted wanted it that way. He wanted to make sure I had time to get Cadee out before they made contact. We weren't sure if we could even get out of the country."

———

"That's what I thought." Barnabas looked around at the men sitting there. "Breck?"

Breck Curran, second in command to Barnabas, looked up. "We can leave this for now. Benen, you and I will talk. I need to talk to Cadee as well. Let's pray we don't overwhelm her in any way when we do. Now, Burney, your team. We need to send you six out to British Columbia. There are some people out there we need to talk to. Your team's up. You'll leave in the morning."

Benen finally stood, stretching. For some reason, it had been a long meeting, many items to discuss. He headed for the door, not seeing the looks following him, intent on finding Cadee.

"Buckley? How is he?" Breck stood beside Buckley.

"To tell you the truth, I really don't know. I need to talk to him and meet Cadee. Maybe this afternoon." He groaned. "No, I can't. I have a couple coming in for counselling."

"Try this evening then. You don't have any meetings?"

Buckley shook his head. "No. This is hard, you know."

"I know. It's tough for us. Think of how it is for them."

"True." Buckley walked away, leaving Breck staring after him, a frown on his face.

Cadee turned from the kitchen sink. She was more stable on her feet, feeling a bit stronger, and had insisted that she would and could get her own breakfast. Benen had laughed at her, dropped a kiss on her cheek and walked away, leaving her staring after him, a hand on her cheek at the spot of the kiss. Now that he was back, she had no idea how to face him.

"Cadee, are you up to a group potluck this weekend?"

"Why?"

"Because we are invited to the potluck here. We usually get together for a meal at least every four or five weeks. We're a little late doing that this time. There's been so much going on."

She shrugged, leaning back against the counter, her arms folded. "I guess. What do we take?"

It was Benen's turn to shrug. "Whatever you want. I usually take a salad and rolls. If you want to do something different, that's good. Just let Anna know. She coordinates us."

"Sounds as if she was dressing you all in different clothing that had to match." She smirked as he laughed. "Now, Benen? What's on for today? You have commitments."

"For this morning. Then we need to head to the bank and get you set up with an account here." He walked towards her and drew her into a hug, feeling her hug him back, finding a crack opening in his heart.

"We can do that. But I do need to shop for some clothes. I don't have winter clothing. I haven't needed thrm."

—

Cadee looked behind her later that afternoon, feeling eyes watching her, but not seeing anyone. But then everyone here was a stranger to her. She turned back to the jacket Benen was holding out, insisting the jade colour was just what she needed. She shrugged. Clothing was clothing, she thought. I don't need special stuff. Just everyday stuff. She paused, as she saw the sweater he had picked out for her, a soft green, knowing he wanted to her buy it, but not sure she should.

"You need these, Cadee. Don't worry about the cost. We can afford these." He studied her and then sighed, telling her what his wage was.

He watched her mouth drop open and then snap closed. Her eyes narrowed as she thought of her own salary.

"And just what will mine be?" Benen told her, reaching out to catch her arm as she swayed. "It can't be that much."

"It is. Trust me. Barnabas and his father considered everything when they set out our wages."

She was jostled by the crowd, not feeling the hand that was quickly stuck into her jacket pocket and then removed, the man disappearing in the crowd without being seen.

Chapter 9

Feeling her jacket pocket later, making sure the pockets were empty before she laundered it, Cadee frowned as she pulled out the folded piece of paper. It wasn't hers, that much she knew. She hadn't put it there.

She unfolded it and read it, her face turning white as she did so. She spun, steadying herself against the wall as her vision clouded for a moment. She needed to find Benen. Only, he wasn't there.

She paused in the lobby of the building, not sure where she should go. She knew he had an office on the main floor, just not where. The paper was clenched in her hand, as she stood in front of the elevators, debating whether to go back up to the apartment or not.

She jumped as a voice spoke beside her and turned, a frown on her face. She didn't know the man standing there.

"Cadee? Are you okay?" Blair Campion, one of the men on Benen's team, watched her closely.

"I'm sorry?"

He grinned. "I'm Blair. I asked if you were okay."

She shook her head. "No, I'm not. I was looking for Benen."

"He's not here. I saw him drive away about an hour ago. Did he not tell you?" Blair's hand under her arm kept her upright.

"He did. I forgot." She stared at the paper in her hand. "I just so needed to talk with him."

Blair reached and gently removed the paper from her hand, a dark frown on his face as he did so. "Where did you get this?"

"In my jacket. We had been shopping. Someone must have slipped it into my jacket. I never saw them. Never felt it."

Blair nodded, his head up, searching. "Come with me. It's okay, Cadee. I just want to head to Branigan's office. He's in and can help you with that."

"But Benen?"

"We'll let him know where you are. It's okay. We don't bite." He grinned as she stared at him for a moment before her mouth snapped closed.

"I need to stop doing that. I'll be catching flies if I don't."

Blair heard her muttering and stared at her in his turn. "What did you just say?"

She looked up, flushing for a moment. "Mom used to tell me to close my mouth or I'd catch flies. Sorry. Old habits of talking to myself die hard."

Blair began to laugh, knowing that Benen had found himself quite a lady. "That's okay. I talk to the cars all the time." He grinned at her again. "I'm a mechanic."

Branigan looked up from his desk as they entered and rose, walking towards them.

"Blair? Cadee?"

Blair handed him the slip of paper even as he seated Cadee in a chair in front of the desk. "Cadee found that in her jacket, she thinks from this afternoon when they were shopping."

Branigan watched Cadee closely, not being familiar with her enough to read her face. "Cadee?"

His voice brought her face up to him and she shook her head. "I'm sorry. I just found it. I don't know who put it there."

Branigan stared at her before he looked down at the paper he held and his face grew stern.

"Cadee?"

She shrugged. "I didn't see who did it. But I wouldn't have known them anyway. I'm a stranger here, remember?" She sank back, her face pale, her strength almost depleted. She didn't hear the tap at the door and then quick footsteps across the floor towards. She didn't see Benen drop to his knees beside her until she felt his arms around her and his voice talking with Branigan.

Her face turned towards him, almost nose to nose with him, as he studied her face, seeing the fatigue in her face and how she was sitting.

"Cadee, darling, what did you go and find?" His words were soft.

She shrugged again. "I don't know, Benen. Just a slip of paper that threatened me." She blinked, her eyes misting with tears that he knew were not like her. She never cried, he thought.

"We'll look into it. Blair brought you to the right person. Branigan is a security expert. He's likely already been doing that." He looked up to see Branigan nodding. "When he finds something, he'll talk to us."

Cadee gave a slow nod, her strength fading, her mind becoming somewhat foggy. "I haven't heard from Mom and Dad."

"No, we haven't, Cadee. They would contact the mission. I spoke with the office about thirty minutes ago. They have heard nothing and should have. I talked to Barnabas. He said he's sending a couple of the guys down that way, to try and trace their tracks."

"Thank him for me." She yawned, her eyes closing as she settled back into the chair. "Wake me up when he calls, please?"

Benen began to chuckle, even as the other men stared at her. "Come on, Cadee, darling. We need to get you back to the apartment. Branigan needs his office, you know."

"No, he doesn't. I can use it." Cadee drifted off even as Benen, laughter sparkling on his face, gathered her close in his arms and rose.

"Did she really just say that?" Branigan asked, a smile lurking on his face.

"She did. She doesn't always make sense when she's tired like this." Benen grinned. "You wouldn't believe some of the conversations we've had over the years."

Blair began to laugh. "I can believe that."

51

Benen stood back from the door early that evening to let Branigan and Buckley enter. He frowned at them before pointing to the living room.

"I'll be right back. Do you need to talk to Cadee?"

The men exchanged a look. "We should, if she's available."

"Let me go see. There's fresh coffee, by the way."

The two men watched him walk down the hall before exchanging glances and then heading for the kitchen, filling mugs with coffee. They stood for a moment, not quite sure about entering the living room before Buckley shrugged and headed that way. He figured Benen knew where he wanted them. He sat, his eyes sliding closed as he prayed, knowing this would be a difficult meeting.

Benen paused for a moment outside the closed door to Cadee's room, his hand on the door itself, his heart praying for his bride. He had seen the looks on his friends' faces and didn't like them. He was afraid for her, afraid for her parents.

He tapped and then opened the door before moving to crouch beside the bed, his hand resting on Cadee's face.

"Cadee? Can you wake?" He waited, a slight smile on his face. "Cadee, darling, I need you to wake up."

Cadee's one eye opened and she glared at him from the pile of blankets she was buried under. "I'm sleeping, Benen. Go away.'

"Sorry, Cadee. I do need you to wake up. Branigan's here and wants to talk to you." He brushed back the hair from her face. "Come on, darling. Rise and shine." He stood, staring down at her for a moment. "Five minutes, or I'll come back and carry you out looking like that."

She continued to glare at him even as she shoved back the blankets. "Go on. I'll be out. I'm up now. You've made such a racket."

Benen laughed as he shut the room door behind him, shaking his head. She hadn't changed, he thought, didn't like to be awakened and told to get up. He leaned against the wall as he waited, his heart in prayer for his lady, not sure what they would be expecting to hear from Branigan. And Buckley here as well.

He turned as the door opened, and Cadee peeked out, a smile on his face as he wrapped her into his arms. "Let's pray first, darling. We'll need it, I suspect."

She nodded against his chest, feeling safe for the first time in months, she thought. Now, where did that thought come from, she wondered?

She watched Branigan closely as she waited for him to speak. Benen had sent her in to sit on the couch and he was just heading back with her tea and his coffee. He set the mugs down before seating himself and then wrapping an arm around her, drawing her close to him. She frowned at him for a moment, thinking he was being bold, and then realized that, no, he really wasn't. They were married, after all, of sorts, and he was always caring and concerned about her. She never had realized that before.

"Buckley, will you pray first? I think we'll need it." Branigan's face was sober, and his words clipped. Benen stared at him, and then down at Cadee, knowing it was not likely to be good news.

"I can." Buckley's voice filled the room as he petitioned for safety, healing, protection and wisdom for the couple in front of him.

Branigan hesitated to speak when Buckley had finished, not quite sure how to proceed.

"Spit it out! That's usually the best way." Cadee's words startled him for a moment before he began to laugh.

"I can do that." He still hesitated, his eyes on Benen, wondering just how to proceed.

"Did you find anything on the note?" Benen's question didn't surprise Branigan.

"Not really. I kept a copy and turned the original over to the detective I spoke with. He'll have his lab take a look at it, but it's down the line as to when it can be done. There's no urgency he said. Yes, there is a threat there against Cadee, but we have no idea or evidence to indicate who or why. He did say that if it was from the country you fled from, Cadee, he may need to talk to the police there."

—

She snorted. "That won't help. There is a lot of corruption, unfortunately, in the force. I couldn't tell him who to talk to that would help." She leaned against Benen, her face sober. "But why me? I don't remember seeing or hearing anything that I shouldn't have."

"It may be something that was so innocent to you hearing it that you have forgotten it. It may be someone who was out of place where you were that you noticed and forget. It may also be an object that you have in your belongings. They're here now and in a storage unit. At some point, we'll have you go through them." He held up a hand as she opened her mouth to speak. "Right now, Doc has said you can't. Not for a couple of days. He said to remind you that you almost died and are still recovering."

She snapped her mouth closed, anger building inside her at the thought. "Yeah, well, there is that, isn't there? I need to do this, Benen. I need to." Her faced turned up to his even as she was pleading, no, begging him to let her go through her belongings. "Please?"

"We'll see how you are in the morning, darling. But I think there's more, isn't there, Branigan?" Benen's eyes never left Cadee's face as he spoke, seeing the fatigue and pain mingling there.

"There is." Branigan didn't speak for a moment, Buckley's eyes shifting between his friends. "We have been looking into where your parents are, Cadee."

She looked at him, hope in her eyes. "They're back? They're here?"

———

55

"No, I'm sorry, Cadee. They're not. We do know they crossed into the neighbouring country and managed to make their way onto a bus. But since then, they seem to have disappeared. We're working on that. I have sent a couple of men down there with Andy to try and trace their whereabouts."

Cadee sat back, devastated that her parents were missing. God, why? You promised to protect us. I'm safe. But are Mom and Dad?

Chapter 11

Moving restlessly through the apartment, Cadee finally stood in the office doorway, watching Benen at work, not wanting to disturb him, but not wanting to be too far away from him. She knew she needed to sort through the feelings she had for him, but not today, she thought. Not today. I need to start going through my stuff, as Dad calls it.

She turned, heading for the living room, and reaching for her Bible. She needed reassurance and confidence from God that He was in control, that He would protect her and her family. Her eyes sought the hallway, hearing Benen's voice, and included him in her prayers.

Benen had looked up as he heard Cadee move away. He had wanted to go to her, to pray with her, but his client was demanding his attention. He finally stood after what seemed too long a time and moved away from his desk. He stretched, his muscles sore from sitting for so long, hands reaching for the ceiling, before he lowered them and tucked his flannel shirt back in. He walked down the hallway, stopping for a moment to watch Cadee as she sat on the couch, legs spread out in front of her under a blanket, her Bible on her lap, her head bent as she read. He headed for the kitchen, squinting at the clock. Lunchtime, he thought, reaching for bread and sandwich fixings, making her tea and his coffee, before he loaded everything on a tray and carried it into the living room, setting her meal before her.

She looked up as he moved her feet, seating where they had rested, and then resting them back on his legs, tucking the blanket around them, and leaving a hand on them for a moment.

"Benen?"

"It's lunchtime, Cadee. Not much for now, but I think you should eat." Benen watched as she sighed, and then nodded, reaching to set her Bible on the table.

Cadee sighed, knowing she needed to eat, but always wanting to fast and pray until her parents were found. She watched Benen from under her eyelashes, knowing he would understand but that he would still push her to eat, given that she had been sick.

"Benen?" When he looked up at her, she continued. "What is it you actually do?"

"I work in IT, problem solving for small companies and individuals. A lot of what I do can be done remotely. I sometimes travel, but not often."

"But someone said you volunteer. Where and why?" She bit into her sandwich, pulling it back to look at it. "You remembered."

"What? That you dislike mustard on your ham and cheese? Of course, I would. We've made too many of them for me to forget." He bit into his own sandwich, his thoughts straying to years earlier, not seeing the surprised but pleased look on her face.

He finally set his place aside and reached for his mug of coffee, watching her face as he did so.

"Cadee? Talk to me."

She shook her head. "What do I say, Benen? You're taking care of me, trying to protect me. I just don't want you keeping anything from me. That's all."

"And I'm not, darling. I'm not. Branigan and the guys are working on stuff." He stared across the room, his eyes on the clock sitting on the fireplace mantle. "We can work on your things, if you like. I just don't want you getting overtired."

"I know." She looked around the room, liking the soft peach he had chosen for the walls, the wooden and leather furniture, the tasteful pictures. "So, tell me. What do you volunteer at?"

He shook his head. "Not giving up on that, are you?" He laughed as she glared at him for a moment. "Cool it, darling. I'm not hiding anything from you. I volunteer at a local camera club, helping the members learn how to properly edit their photos."

She stared at him and then at the photos. "Those are yours?"

"They are."

"Nice." She moved restlessly. "Have you heard anything on Mom and Dad?"

"Not yet. Barnabas said it might take a couple of days for the guys to find out anything." He lifted her feet to the floor, standing with a hand out to help her stand before he gathered their dishes and carried them back to the kitchen and the dishwasher.

"I can't get used to all these conveniences." Cadee stood and watched him as he worked. "We didn't have all this before Mom and Dad left for the mission."

"No, you didn't." Benen paused, before he turned to her. "How did they come to go out?"

She shrugged, her hands in her sweater pockets. "I don't really know. I know they wanted to when I was young. I came home one day to find out they had applied and been accepted. I was at a loss. This was right after college. I applied to work in the office down there as well."

"Didn't you have to fundraise or find support?"

She shrugged again. "We did to a certain extent. But we were told that someone had offered to sponsor us, so we didn't have to raise a lot." She frowned, before a distressed look crossed her face. "Benen? Who would do that?"

"They didn't tell you who?"

She shook her head. "No. Whoever it was wanted to remain anonymous, but we were told it was specific to us." She looked up, sudden fear on her face. "Benen? What if it was a set up to get us down there for some reason?"

"We'll talk to Barnabas. He knows the mission board you went out under. He'll see what he can find out. It has now become a matter of life and death for all of you.

She shuddered, his arms going around her. "I'm scared, Benen. Scared for Mom and Dad." Her voice was barely above a whisper.

His heart breaking for his bride, Benen wrapped her into his arms and prayed for her and her parents.

Chapter 12

Benen stood at the entry to his storage unit, staring at the few boxes inside. He had no idea where Cadee's parents belongings had ended up. Here, he thought, but he wasn't sure. He wrapped an arm around Cadee and pulled her tight to him, his eyes dropping to her face, a sigh suppressed at the look on her face.

"We'll take our time, darling. If it's too much, we'll stop and come back. Doc told me to watch you. It's not been that long since we almost lost you."

She nodded, her hand wrapping around his, tightening with her emotions. "I know. And that I don't get. Why me?"

"We'll figure it out. Barnabas sent a text message a bit ago. He's onto something and wants to talk with us later."

"Has he heard anything?" She looked up, hope in her eyes.

"He didn't say." Benen studied the boxes. "Where do you want to start?"

"I'm not sure." She moved away, stopping to stare down at the first box. "This is Mom and Dad's." She looked around. "It's not much to show for a lifetime, is it? They sold off just about everything before they went out. I think they put some boxes in a friend's attic, but I'm not even sure they're still in there. Mom said something a couple of years ago of moving them, sorting through them again, and getting rid of anything that didn't matter."

She knelt, reaching for the box, finding Benen's hand there with his pocket knife to slit the tape, and then reaching to fold back the flaps for her. She hesitated, reaching for a moment to rub at her eyes, before she picked up the first thing, a picture of the three of them. She handed it to Benen, whose took it, his eyes on her.

She continued to look through the box, even as he too examined each item she handed him, pulling the pictures apart to search inside the frame.

"Benen?" Her soft question had his head coming up. "Why look inside?"

"Just in case something has been put in there." He stopped for a moment, sitting back on the floor, his eyes on her. "Would you recognize something that's not your parents?"

"I don't know. I would hope I would. Unless it was something that they had hidden away and not shown me." She paused, deep in thought. "About a year ago, Dad was acting strange. I thought it was because they had just come back from a neighbouring country where they had been to a conference. Maybe it was more."

"Give Branigan the details. He'll find someone to look into it." He reached for the next box as she tidily packed away the first one.

Two hours later, she reached for the last box, one of her, her hands hesitating, fear suddenly running through her. She moved back, on her feet, her arms wrapping around herself. Benen had stepped out of the room to take a call and stood where he could watch her, wanting to go to her but unable to end his call with a client. He nodded as Brady moved past him into the room.

"Cadee?" Brady's voice startled her.

"I'm sorry." She spun, her eyes huge as she studied him.

"Sorry, Cadee. I'm Brady. I don't think we've had an opportunity to meet." He reached out to shake her hand.

"No, I don't think we have." She sighed. "There are just too many of you. I'll never keep your names all straight."

"Sure you will. It's easy. We all have the same initials as Barnabas." He began to laugh as her eyes seemed to grow in size. "That's it. All our first names start with B and our last names start with C. Barnabas had a reason for that. He'll explain it if you ask."

"I just might." She studied the box in front of her.

"Something wrong with that box?"

She nodded as she looked up at Brady. "There is. I felt evil in it. And I shouldn't."

His face growing stern, Brady crouched down beside it. "It's the same box you packed?"

"I think so. Why?"

"Because it looks as if the original tape was removed and then the box re-taped." He looked up at her, seeing Benen walking towards them as he

---

pocketed his phone. "Benen? I think this is the box you might be looking for."

"Is it? Then how be we take it to the conference room. Blair said they had set up in there." Benen reached for the box, finding Brady's hands there first, Brady's head nodding at Cadee.

"Come on, Cadee darling. We're moving to a conference room. We can spread out what's in this box." Benen reached for her hand, waiting as she stood still. "Cadee? Anything else?"

She finally shook her head before pulling her hand free and walking away, deep in thought.

"Something more is going on with her, Benen." Brady's assessment of her told him that.

"I know. I can't get her to talk. That's not her. At least the her I know." Benen sighed deeply as he moved forward, locking the storage room door, and then reaching to wrap an arm around Cadee, finding her shaking. "Cadee?"

She looked up at him, fear on her face. "There's something in there, Benen. I don't know what, but I can feel the evil from it. I don't want to know, but I have to, no, need to know."

Benen carefully opened the box, Cadee standing away from it, her eyes on his hands. Brady stood near him, ready to take the articles from Benen as he emptied the box. Brady laid them down carefully, then reached to take the box from Benen, searching it carefully, frowning as he found an envelope under one of the bottom flaps. He stared at it, seeing no name or any writing on the envelope before he touched Benen's arm, holding out the paper for him to take.

Benen looked at it, then at Cadee as he heard an exclamation from her, dropping the envelope to scoop her into his arms as her eyes closed and her body dropped suddenly towards the floor.

Chapter 13

Brady pointed to a chair, moving quickly in. As a paramedic, he understood how shock could work on a body, and knowing what she had been through, he was concerned. He looked around as he heard footsteps, and Bradon Cahill and his dog, Kade, appeared.

"Bradon? Is Doc around?"

"No, he said he's on duty at the clinic. Do you need something?"

"Yeah. The kit from the infirmary. I don't want to move her yet, if I can help it. And some blankets. I need to lay her flat."

Bradon was off on a run before Brady had quite finished, returning in short order, shoving the kit Brady wanted at him, then spreading blankets on the floor, stepping back as Benen gathered Cadee into his arms, finding her rousing and fighting him. He sat back into the chair, keeping her close to him, his voice a mere whisper.

Brady crouched in front of her, concern on his face. "Benen, you're old friends. Has this ever happened before?"

Benen thought for a moment. "Not that I'm aware of. But she's been through too much already. When does it end?"

Brady nodded, stethoscope in his hand, as he paused. "I need to assess her vitals, Benen."

"Go ahead. I'll make sure you can." He looked down at Cadee, seeing her eyes opening. "Cadee, darling, Brady needs to check you out, make sure you're fine."

"Brady? Who's he? Where am I?" She stared at Benen. "Benen? Don't we have to pack up everything? Dad said we needed to leave in the morning." She stared around, jumping at the close proximity of Brady and then jumping again as she felt a tongue on her hand, staring at Kade. "Who are these?"

"We're home, Cadee. You had an adventure that took a few years off my life. It's been about a week or so." Benen watched as she thought through that and then nodded.

"What happened?" When he paused, he felt the anger in her, anger that he knew was not normal for her.

"When we were heading for the airplane, you received what you thought was a bug bite but the doctors think was a tiny dart full of poison. I almost lost you, darling."

She stared at him for a moment, before looking down at her hand. "We really did that, didn't we?"

"We did, Cadee. We did. Your dad thought it was the only way."

She nodded before she laid her head down on his shoulder. "Thank you. I'm sure Dad was right. He was disturbed the last month or so, but wouldn't tell Mom and I why. He was afraid for us, wouldn't let us go out anywhere on our own. He had men and youths from the church guarding our home. Did he say why?"

Benen shook his head in turn. "He didn't. He said we'd talk when we reached a safer place."

"Where are they, Benen? They're in danger, aren't they? I can feel that. I wish they had waited and come with us."

"I wanted them to. They slipped away on us when we were cleaning up the kitchen. Your Dad seemed to think you needed to come back first." He sighed as he exchanged a look with Brady and Bradon, who stood watching, grim looks on their faces. "The last thing he said to me was to watch you closely. Someone had put out a contract on you, and he didn't know why."

"A contract?" She gave an unbelieving laugh. "Benen? Why? I worked in the office at the mission. I didn't see anything I shouldn't have. I was very careful with the people I met, where I went, who I was with. Again, why?"

"That we don't know. Your Dad might but he hasn't got here yet. I think they've gone into hiding, darling. Some of our guys are down there right now, trying to find them."

"They won't unless he wants them to. He had made plans, told us about them, but we didn't believe him. I guess he was right after all." She shoved at his arms, rising, and walking to the table, her hands touching the objects laying there. "There are all trinkets they picked up down there. It's strange that they were all in one box."

"I think your Dad packed this one." Benen stood behind her, his arms around her. "I think he put these together for a reason. We have to figure it out."

She nodded, her head rubbing against his chin, before she stared at the envelope. "That's what I felt, Benen. That's what I felt." Her memory rushed back, engulfing her in a violent storm of shaking. "What is in it?"

Brady took a look at her and left the room on the run, knowing they needed Buckley there. Buckley looked up from his desk and the notes he was working on for his Sunday sermon, rose and ran after Brady without asking any questions.

Buckley stood beside Cadee, his eyes on her, before he looked up at Benen.

"Benen?"

"There's something about that envelope that is scaring Cadee badly. We need to bath her in prayer, for protection, for safety."

Buckley simply bowed his head and prayed, asking for that from the God who he knew was in control   of   all.

Chapter 14

Pulling out the flap on the envelope, Benen hesitated for a moment before he handed it to Buckley.

"Buckley? Would you, please?"

Buckley stared down at the letter and then up at Benen before his eyes shifted to Cadee, who was staring at the envelope. "You're sure?"

She looked up, an unreadable expression on her face. "Please. I can't."

Buckley pulled out the folded paper inside, feeling what she had felt, unfolding it and then frowning. "It's in another language. Can you read it, Cadee?"

She leaned over as far as she could from the safety of Benen's arms and then nodded. "I can. It's not nice." She spun, her arms around Benen, fear, no, terror shaking her body.

Benen stared down at her. "Is Brenden here?" Brenden Conroy was a interpreter.

"No, but Brennen is." Buckley looked around as he heard the door softly closed. "Brady's gone for him. Benen, get her sitting down and something hot into her."

Bradon set a tray of hot drinks of the table at that point. "I figured we'd need something." He turned to look behind him. "Anna's on her way and she has Berneen with her. Is that okay?"

Benen hesitated and then nodded. "That should be okay, I guess." He drew Cadee down into a chair, crouching down beside her, his arm around her, his hand on hers. "Cadee?"

She finally turned to look at him, and he drew in a sharp breath at the look in her eyes, one he had never seen before

"They're not in hiding, are they? They're missing? He has them!"

"Who has them?" All eyes were on her before they looked around at one another, Anna and Berneen walking in at that point and halting, not quite sure what they had walked in on.

"He does. I don't know his name. He used to come to church and then to the house to talk to Dad. Dad never liked him. He made sure Mom and I were never visible when the man came around." She looked up at Benen again before poking at the paper Buckley still held. "He threatened me in that. He said I had something of his I needed to give him. I don't. I would remember if I did. And I don't." She looked up at Benen again before throwing herself at him, only Buckley's hand on his back stopping him from falling backwards. "It's all my fault. It's my fault they're missing."

"Tell me exactly what the letter says." Benen looked up at Brennen entered the room, concern on his face for his friend and his wife

"Benen? Brady said you had a letter you needed translated?"

Buckley handed it to him. "Cadee has basically told us it threatens her and asks for something she says she doesn't have."

Brennen studied it and nodded. "That's quite a condensed version of what it says. There's a whole lot more to it, isn't there, Cadee?" His voice sounded harsh, but that was the concern he felt coming through.

She threw her head back to stare at him, their looks duelling with one another, before she nodded. "There is. Benen, they threaten to kill Mom and Dad, say they know where they are and that they can get to them at any time. They threaten you, telling me they'll kill you if I don't turn over the object to them. They know where I am and have threatened Barnabas and everyone else here. They said they can reach out to any one of us and harm us. I have to turn over whatever it is in the next two days." She didn't look away from Brennen as she spoke. "I have no idea what it is, so how can I?"

"So, we go through what we've pulled out of the box." Benen rose, his hand resting on her head in a caress. "Buckley, we'll need to pull that box apart as well. When did they put in that letter?"

"Who knows? It wasn't after it got here, that's for sure." Brennen pointed with the mug he held. "She's pretty much put it into a nutshell, but it's a lot worse sounding that what she says."

"Can you write out the translation? Let Barnabas know and then whoever is working on this."

"We all are, Benen." Brennen paused in setting his mug down. "You know right well that we are all involved. We can't do anything less than that."

Benen turned as he felt Cadee rising, moving to stand near Berneen. He couldn't hear their soft conversation, but he could see Cadee relaxing some.

"Anna, when is the dinner?" Buckley spoke up.

"Sunday after church. That two days from now. Got your sermon ready yet?" Anna, Doc's wife, grinned at Buckley as he shook his head. "I know you do. It's always ready by now. You just refine it."

"And does everyone know what they're to bring?" Buckley's smile widened as Anna shook a finger at him.

"What we always do. You know that, Buckley." She paused, her china cup of tea in her hand, as she studied the items on the table. "Some of this is really bizarre, isn't it?" She looked around, then called for Cadee. "Cadee, can you come here? I know you don't want to, but these things won't hurt you. You need to talk to us, tell us what you know about them."

Cadee moved towards her, her hands once more touching the objects. "This one. I have never seen it before. I've seen the others. Dad collected them from artisans down there. But this one? I have no idea what it is."

Benen reached to take it from her. "I do. It's an pestle, used in their cooking. But why would your father have it?"

———

73

Brady reached for it, his face paling as he did. "I've done some reading on poisoned darts. This could well have been something that was used in the preparation of the poison."

Cadee paled and moved away. "What did Dad go and do?"

Chapter 15

Benen quietly shut the bedroom door he had opened and walked away. Cadee was sleeping at last, he thought, knowing he would be back there to check on her. It was late evening, and he had not been able to settle down to his work, and he needed to do that. He sighed, reaching to pour yet another cup of coffee, and then walking through to his office, sinking into his chair, exhausted beyond belief. He reached for his phone and then reached past it for his Bible. He needed some God time, time to refresh his heart and soul with verses about trusting God, about God's protection.

He finally rose, heading for the kitchen to rinse out his mug and set the coffee for the morning, and then turning out lights as he moved through the apartment, standing at the living room window, the room dark behind him, staring out at the night, searching the heavens and the bright stars, feeling God's peace in his heart, but knowing their troubles were far from over.

He finally turned, reaching to close the drapes, not seeing the two men standing in the shadows of the trees that lined the parking lot, their eyes on his windows before they too walked away.

He showered, finding clean towels and clean pyjamas waiting for him. He felt them, knowing that Cadee had done that, taking care of him. He smiled and then, dressing, turning to walk to her bedroom door, tapping lightly before he entered and crouched down beside her, his heart breaking at the tears on her face before he kissed a cheek and rose, heading for his own bed and sleep.

He awoke in the night, his head raising, listening, before he was on his feet and running for Cadee, his bare feet hitting the floor hard at each step. Hand to the door knob, he twisted it, throwing it open, the light from the hall shining into the room. He paused for a moment not seeing her before he saw the doors to the walk-in closet open. He hastened across the room, pausing for a moment to search for her, finding her huddled into a corner, her arms wrapped around herself as she wept.

He dropped down beside her, reaching to catch her to him, his arms strong around her, his heart breaking at her sobs. When she finally settled down, he spoke.

"Cadee? What happened?"

"A bad dream! A nightmare! I dreamt Mom and Dad were dead. They had been killed." She shuddered even as she spoke, her voice hoarse.

Benen's heart broke for his bride and he began to pray, pray as he never had before. She finally stirred after a while, shoving at him and then to her feet, to pace the bedroom even as he watched, a shoulder leaning against the closet door, an eye on the clock. Only two in the morning. They both needed to sleep. He finally approached her, standing in her way, causing her to stop and raise her face to stare at him. He simply swept her into his arms and walked from the room, settling her down into his place on his bed and pulling up the covers.

"Benen? What are you doing?" Cadee tried to rise but his hand on her shoulder kept her still.

"You need to sleep. You won't sleep in there. I know that. Not tonight. So you sleep here." He rose, heading for his closet, finding a blanket, and then covering himself as he stretched out beside her, his arms reaching to pull her close. "Go to sleep, darling. I'll keep watch for a while and God will watch over us both."

They slept, not knowing that in less than a week, their world would be turned upside down in a way neither one of them expected.

———

Chapter 16

Sunday morning found Benen and Cadee standing outside the church, her hand tight in his, even as she hesitated about moving forward.

"They'll judge me, Benen. I just know they will. We married too quickly. They don't know me." Her voice rose in panic even as his hand squeezed hers.

"Benen? Who do you have here you're not letting go off?" The older gentleman stopped, his hand on Benen's shoulder, a look of interest on his face.

"Jace, this is my wife, Cadee. Cadee, darling, this is the trustee board chair, Jace Enger." Benen watched as Jace stared at him and then Cadee.

"Took a page from Baird's book, did you, son, and didn't let the love of your life escape?" He laughed, before he reached to hug Cadee, surprising her. "Welcome to our church family, Cadee. We don't bite, at least not much. Benen, you and your bride must join Martha and I for dinner one night this week. Martha'll be in touch." He walked away, leaving Cadee staring after him, her mouth open until Benen gently tapped her chin.

"They're mostly like that. They welcome you in as a family member." He walked her into the church, finding a seat beside Berneen and Baird, letting Cadee sit next to Berneen. He looked around,

—

a frown on his face for a moment, feeling someone watching him but now seeing anyone.

"Feel that too, do you?" Baird spoke quietly over the heads of the two women.

"I do. I know what you mean now." He listened to the sermon Buckley brought and his eyes frequently sought Cadee's face, seeing the thoughtfulness his words brought to her.

They walked away from the church, heading for home, having decided to walk that morning, not seeing some of the men following them.

"He's good, Benen."

"He is, Cadee. I have learned more from him that I have any minister I have sat under. He encourages us to search the Bible, to prove what he says. He wants to know if we are in disagreement with his messages and he'll spend time talking them through. We have some interesting discussions at times."

"Dad will like him." A troubled look flitted across her face. "You said the men are back from down there?"

"They are. Barnabas wants to have a meeting tomorrow with us all. You as well. You know the area, so perhaps you'll bring a different perspective to what they say."

"Oh, I'm sure I will. I just don't know the area Mom and Dad fled to." She sighed, her head resting against his arm for a moment. "It's hard, Benen. Very hard. I feel like I abandoned them down there, even though they left us."

—

"I know, darling. I know you do."

Seated at last in another conference room, this one set up with a kitchen, and with the potluck set up as a buffet, Cadee listened as Doc asked a blessing on their meal. She poked at her food at first before she began to eat, listening to the conversation and teasing around her, Berneen sitting beside her by choice, asking her questions, some of which Cadee's missed.

Brady finally looked across the table at her. "Cadee? Did you do this kind of stuff when you were young? Like at church?"

She shrugged. "Not really. The church we went to was huge, so we didn't have many meals, other than a formal Christmas dinner." She turned her head to Benen. "I don't know that many of the people really associated with one another."

He shook his head. "I don't think they did. Yours was a very formal church. Your family never seemed to fit in."

She sighed. "We didn't. I hated it. The youth group was brutal."

"It was, that I can remember, even though the leaders tried."

"They tried, but failed, miserably. I finally quit going. There was too much competition there."

"Competition? What do you mean?" Berneen leaned forward, eager to hear Cadee's response.

"I guess I mean with personalities. A lot of the girls were only interested in catching one of the guy's eyes, especially the popular ones." She smirked at Benen. "You never noticed or knew, did you?"

"Knew what?" He was puzzled, not sure what she meant.

"Benen! How could you not? You didn't see them throwing themselves at you?"

The table had silenced, waiting to hear his response.

"No, I didn't. I wasn't interested in ladies at the time. I was too busy with my studies." He stared at her, his eyes narrowing as she began to laugh. "You find this funny?"

"I do." She shared a look with Berneen who began to laugh as well, thinking she knew where Cadee was heading with her words.

"Why?" He took a bite of his apple pie, his eyes on her.

"Because they all wanted to be your girl, to date you." She smirked once more. "And I did it."

"Did what?"

"I'm your girl."

The members of the group began to laugh at the expression on her face.

"She's got you there, Benen." Doc reached to wipe tears of laughter from his face. "She really does have you, doesn't she?"

Benen reached to hug her, dropping a kiss on her cheek. "You always did, darling. You always did." His voice was low enough that only she could hear him, causing her to stare at him in wonder.

—

Barnabas was on a search. He needed to talk to both Benen and Cadee and could find neither one. He stood in the lobby of the building, rubbing at his cheek, looking around before finally heading outside, shrugging into his jacket. It's winter, he thought, but not cold. It feels more like early spring than mid-December. He paused, knowing Christmas was coming, but with Benen in whatever it was he was involved with, he wasn't sure how to plan the usual Christmas dinner. He would leave it to Amy and Anna, making sure that Berneen and Cadee were involved in the planning if that was what they wanted to do.

He searched the buildings outside, not finding them before he headed to the large building that housed the gym. He knew Benen liked to work out, but wasn't sure about Cadee. He stopped, realizing he knew very little about her after all.

He cracked the door open, hearing the sound of equipment in use and laughter, both men and women. He stepped through the door, finding Berneen and Cadee walking the track, the men on the equipment, Berneen's teasing voice raised to be heard over the sounds. He stood for a moment, watching before Berneen saw him and waved.

Benen sat up on the weight bench he had been laying on, Brady spotting him, before he rose, reaching for a towel and then heading for Cadee, his hand coming out automatically to take hers before he walked towards Barnabas.

"Barnabas? You looking for us?" Benen's voice was quiet, holding questions he didn't voice.

"I am, Benen. Are you tied up for the next couple of hours?"

Benen glanced at his watch. "Not until about 11. Then I have to call a client." He pushed open the door. "Let me change and I'll meet you there. Cadee?"

"I'm fine. Hurry. I think Barnabas is in a rush."

The two men stared at her until they saw the sparkle of mirth in her eyes and began to laugh, walking quickly to the main building.

Cadee wandered the conference room, stopping in front of the objects still sitting on the table. She hesitated once more as she searched them, reaching for a small clay box, a frown on her face.

Barnabas looked up from where he was sitting, then rose, walking to stand beside her.

"You seem fascinated by this box." He pointed at it.

"I am. I don't remember that I've seen it before. It's not something Mom or Dad would have had." She reached to remove the lid, Barnabas' hand stopping her.

"I think we'll have someone look at that before you open it." He looked around, finding a large manila envelope and gently removing the box from her hand and inserting into the envelope. "I have a friend who can look at that for you." He wrote on the envelope, before he clicked his pen closed and set it down. "Cadee? How are you doing? Really?"

She shrugged, turning to watch the door, wanting Benen there. She wasn't comfortable talking to Barnabas, and she just didn't know why.

"I'm not sure. I just want my parents here." She saw Benen heading her way, and sighed. This was not how she pictured being married, not as a newlywed, anyway.

Benen paused for a moment, his arm around Cadee, a question on his face.

"Cadee found a small box she didn't recognize. I'm sending it to a friend to have them take a look at it." Barnabas pointed to where he had been sitting. "Let's sit. Brenden and Brandon will be here in just a few moments."

"They have news?" Benen sat into a chair beside Cadee, hope on his face.

"I'm not sure. They got in late Saturday and wanted time to go over what they found before they spoke with you two." He looked down at his notes. "Cadee, have you thought of anything or anyone at all that you could name, tell us about?"

She shook her head, then paused, a frown on her face. "About six or seven weeks ago, there was a letter that came to Dad, from somewhere in that country. He was with me when the mail came and took it from me before I could open it. He was really quiet and withdrawn for a few days after that."

"Did he say what it was about?" Barnabas shared a look with Benen.

"No, he didn't." She rubbed a finger along the edge of the table. "That's when he started talking of taking a furlough. I didn't think he meant it."

Benen's face was thoughtful, Barnabas watching him closely.

"Benen?"

Benen shook his head, bringing himself back to the present. "That's when he wrote to me, Barnabas, asking if I could come down there." A pained look crossed his face even as Cadee turned to look up at him. "He knew, Cadee. He knew then what he would ask of us. He knew I wouldn't and couldn't say no to coming and seeing all of you."

Cadee sat back, her hand going to her mouth, distress on her face. "Dad planned this? He planned for us to marry?" Her head shaking in denial, she turned, ready to rise and run, when Benen spoke.

"He did, Cadee. I am sure he did. You're his little girl, his daughter. No matter that you are a grown woman, he was still that worried about you. He could have chosen anyone. He could have taken a chance and sent you home on your own or with your mother. He was that scared. I saw it. I didn't know why and he wouldn't say."

"But it's not fair to you, Benen. You should have been able to choose your own wife."

Barnabas watched the two closely, not sure if he should leave and let them work it out on their own, or

---

85

stay and support them. He made to shove his chair back, pausing as Benen spoke.

"I did, Cadee, my darling. I did. I could have said no, but I didn't." His heart was in his eyes as she turned, her eyes on him, wonder growing on her face. "We'll talk, my darling. We'll talk. Your Dad knew, I think. Right now, you need to digest what you've learned, and I think Barnabas has things he needs to talk to us about."

Chapter 18

Barnabas stared down at the papers in front of him, conflicted for a moment, his head raising as the door opened and Brenden and Brandon entered, dropping their files on the table before heading to grab mugs of coffee for themselves, and the others as well, setting a cup of tea in front of Cadee, before sliding into chairs opposite the young couple.

"Barnabas? I think we need to pray and pray earnestly right now." Brenden's voice was tired and they could see the lines of fatigue in his face.

"Not a problem. I would have, anyway."

Once they had raised their heads again, Brenden's gaze was on Cadee, who hadn't look up, her thoughts far away, or as far away as the man sitting beside her, his hand on hers, clasping hers tightly. She hadn't known how he felt and to hear him voice what he had, it had shaken her,

"Cadee? Brenden needs to talk to you." Benen's words caught her attention and she looked up and across the table.

"Brenden?"

"Cadee, we did find your parents. They had hidden themselves away." He watched with compassion as she turned to Benen, her arms around him, hiding her face against him as she wept. He blinked back tears from his own eyes as he suspected the rest of them were also doing. He rose, heading for the bathroom off the room and returning with a warm damp cloth he handed to Benen.

She finally raised her head. "They're safe? They're okay?" Hope rose in her face.

"They are." He looked down for a moment before he looked up at her, hoping to reassure her. "They were followed from their home and had to make some quick decisions. They took the bus, but got off before they reached their destination, hoping to avoid being seen. They found a friend who has them safe, setting them to watch for someone looking for them. They found us. We have spoken with that person, but not them. We didn't think it safe for them to do so." He paused to let her compose herself. "That person had a letter from them for you."

Cadee watched as the envelope was pushed across the table to her, her hand resting on it, before she looked up.

"They're okay?" She repeated herself, needing that reassurance.

"For now, they are. We've sent word we'll get them out. We're working on a time frame for that." Brandon looked at Barnabas. "Barnabas, we'll need Andy."

"That's a given. We'll talk." Barnabas looked down at his notes. "Were you able to find out any information on who or why?"

"The person we talked to didn't give us any information but from what they didn't say, your father knows, Cadee. And this person not named is very dangerous and has a far reach. He is concerned about your safety even here, and that of Benen, and then the rest of us." Brandon sat back, his eyes on Benen, watching the emotions roil over his face.

"I figured that out. What else?" Cadee didn't take her eyes from the men across from her.

"He may have said something in that letter. That was the impression we were given. As to getting them out, we'll receive a text message when it's the right time." Brenden paused and pulled out his phone, a soft groan rising from him, as he read the message. "Barnabas, we need to head back today. Is Andy available?"

"He is. He's hanging around all day, suspecting this." Barnabas nodded at the two. "Just you two or do you want others?"

"I think just us." Brenden looked over at Cadee. "I'm sorry, Cadee. We need to leave now. I wish I could stay and help relieve your worries."

She nodded before her eyes dropped to the envelope. "Barnabas? You said you needed to talk to us."

"I do, Cadee. It won't take long." He sighed to himself, not sure how to proceed given what had just happened. "It was about your parents. It seems that the mission they were out with has been taken over without any of the donors being aware of it. All the missionaries, except your parents, have been recalled in the last two months and told the mission is folding. Your parents were the only ones not told. They were led to believe there was nothing wrong, that it was business as usual."

Benen's hand tightened on Cadee. "Then, who are they after? Cadee or her parents?"

<hr>

"Cadee. We need to find out why. And we need to come up with a plan for protecting her." Barnabas raised his hand as she went to protest. "You're family now, Cadee. We take care of our family. Your parents are as well. The guys will bring them here. Anna and Amy will set up an apartment for them to use. Is this what you want, to have them here?"

Overcome with her emotions and unable to speak, Cadee simply nodded. She rose abruptly, her letter in her hand, and almost ran from the room, Benen standing and staring after her.

"She'll be okay, Benen. Go to her." Barnabas stood as well.

Benen shook his head. "She needs a few minutes. She always does if her emotions get the better of her." He looked down at the fingers he was rubbing together, his thoughts muddled.

"Did you mean that?" Barnabas' quiet question raised Benen's head to watch his friend.

"Mean what?"

"What you told her. That you had made your own choice."

Benen nodded, a softened look coming over his face. "I did and I do. She's always been the one. I never saw the other girls, just her. I think that's why I kept in touch with her parents, not her. I was planning on going down there on my next vacation in the summer. I just didn't plan on this."

Barnabas laughed. "No, I don't think you did, but God did. He knew she needed someone to protect

her. And that someone had to be a person she knows
well. You are he, Benen."

Cadee pushed the envelope around on the kitchen table, not willing to open it but also not willing to set it aside. She was torn and conflicted by her emotions. Knowing that the guys were heading back down to find her parents and bring them home added to the mix. She knew Benen had returned, he had stopped, a hand on her shoulder, a kiss on the top of her head before he walked away and to his office.

She grabbed the envelope up quickly and ran to find him, halting in his office doorway as he sat, watching that very spot, hoping and praying that she would come to him. He rose, his arms open to wrap her into a hug as she threw herself at him.

He drew her down with him on the couch he had in the office, an arm around her.

"Cadee?"

"I can't open this, Benen. Why not?" She shoved the letter at him. "You do it."

"You're sure?"

She nodded. "Please. I need you to read it first."

He nodded, his finger finding the flap to unseal the letter, pulling out the folded paper, and frowned. "Your Dad didn't write much, Cadee. There's only one sheet and that is only used on one side."

She gave a small smile. "Dad has become very concise lately, only saying what he really needs to." She pointed at it. "Aren't you going to read it?"

"I will." He unfolded the paper and scanned it, his face paling as he did so.

"Benen? You went white. What did Dad say?" She reached for the letter as he moved it away from her.

"Cadee, your Dad has basically said what Brenden said. He doesn't know the name of the man who has put out the contract on you. He is working on that. He has an idea but needs to be back here to find out more information. He thinks the man is connected with the mission and from this province."

"That's not good. He didn't say who?"

"No. It seems as if he knows but doesn't want to tell you. Not yet. He said he would talk to you when he saw you."

She reached again for the letter, reading it before she frowned and then read it aloud.

"Cadee, girl

"Your life is still at risk. You need to take extra precautions. Stay close to Benin. He will keep you safe.

"Your mother and I are on our way back, but the man looking for you is in Ontario. I won't give his name until we see you and even then I am not sure of it. He may be connected with the mission.

"Father."

She frowned once more. "That's not Dad's handwriting. It's close but it's not. And he never calls me girl, or refers to Mom as mother or himself as father." She looked up at Benen. "And your name is spelt wrong. This is bizarre."

Benen took the letter from her. "That's that then, isn't it?" He reached for his phone he had set on the table in front of him. "I need to alert Barnabas."

Barnabas sat back in his chair, his eyes on the couple, before he reached for his own phone. He had been on his way to their apartment when Benen had called.

"Brenden? Where are you ? About halfway, you say? Cadee and Benen read the letter. It's not from her father. What's that? You know? How? Okay. What was that?" Barnabas' eyes were on Cadee as he listened. "You're landing when? No, that's fine. We'll see you when you get back."

Barnabas pocketed his phone, deep in thought, his eyes on the floor, before he looked over at Cadee.

"Brenden and Brandon are on their way back. They went to where they had found out your parents were at. They had already left. Apparently someone found them and they ran. Brenden's not able to say where they are."

Cadee leaned against Benen, feeling his arm tighten around her. "So, where are they?"

"That we don't know. Brenden and Brandon are working on that. Andy's been stopping at out of the way airports for them to search. If they find them, they'll bring them with them." He watched Benen closely. "They won't be in until late tonight or early tomorrow morning."

"Have they any idea where Mom and Dad are?" Cadee was desperate for news on her parents.

"No, but he says they seem to be moving fast. He suspects they have help." He looked at Benen. "In fact, he seemed to think they may have found a flight."

Benen nodded. "I would suspect that. But does it land in Canada or the United States?"

"I would say the States, as near to the border as they could get."

Chapter 20

Hearing her name called, Cadee spun the next morning as she walked through the lobby with Benen, intent on heading out to town. She stopped, her hands on her mouth, and then she was running across the lobby, to throw herself into the arms of the woman who stood there, the man with her wrapping both women into a hug. Benen stood in shock and was then across the lobby, his hand out to shake the man's. Brandon and Brenden entered behind them, standing just inside the door, fatigue evident in their stance and on their faces, dropping their duffle bags to the floor.

"Mom! Dad! How?" Cadee looked around her mother towards the two men and then ran to hug them as well. "Brandon? Brenden? You found them?"

"Not really. It's more like they found us. They were at the airport when we landed, not sure where to head from there. I think they have quite a story to tell, but they need to rest first." Brandon turned her back towards her parents. "We'll talk, Cadee. Benen. Right now, these two people need to find somewhere to rest and also find some food."

Cadee's arm around her mother, she led her to the elevator, hearing her father's footsteps beside her, and then Benen's rapid steps as he hastened to catch up with them. She searched her parents' faces, seeing the deep-rooted fatigue in them and also the worry in their eyes. Why, Lord? What did they go through that You protected them from?

Hearing Ted talking with Benen in the kitchen, she led her mother to the spare room, taking a deep breath.

"You two can have this room." She rushed to gather her belongings, almost running to dump them into the master bedroom. "It's fine, Mom." Her words were low as her mother went to protest. "It's just for now. Barnabas said they'd arrange an apartment here for you."

Mary stopped her daughter with a hand to her back. "Cadee?"

Cadee shook her head. "It's okay, Mom. We're talking." She turned her face to her mother, a slight smile on it. "It's okay. He told me I was his choice all along."

Mary breathed a sigh of relief, glad that at least one thing in her daughter's life was going as it should. "He always did, Cadee. I could see it in how he looked at you and treasured you. So could your father. Ted told me that's the only reason he asked that of him, suspecting how he felt. And I know from watching you that he's the only one for you."

Cadee gave a slow nod before she hugged her mother. "We'll need to talk. Let's get some food into you two and then you sleep. You'll need it. Tomorrow is sufficient to find out what happened."

"Actually, Cadee, it's not, but it will have to be." Her father's voice had her spinning to face the doorway, seeing the distress on his face and the fear in Benen's eyes.

"Dad?" Cadee moved towards him, finding herself wrapped into his hug, before he turned her towards Benen.

"Let your Mom and I sleep for a bit. We need it. We're not thinking clearly right now." He nodded towards Benen. "Go on with what you had planned for the day. Benen said he'd talk to Barnabas and see if we can meet in the morning. It will take a while to tell our tale."

Benen led Cadee towards the outside door, her hand tight in his. "He's right, darling. Let them sleep. We'll have a chance to talk."

He paused their walk through the lobby, his eyes on Barnabas and Breck as they walked towards them.

"Benen?" Breck's voice was hopeful.

"They're getting ready to settle down and sleep. They've asked if we can meet tomorrow."

Barnabas and Breck exchanged glances, having already spoken with Brenden and Brandon.

"That shouldn't be a problem. I'll call a full meeting of all the guys. They need to hear firsthand what's going on." Breck spoke up. "Cadee, is there anything your parents need today?"

She shrugged. "I have no idea. I didn't see any luggage with them."

"There wasn't." Breck shared a look with Benen. "Brandon said they had nothing with them."

"Then, I'll need to shop for them, to get them some things." Cadee chewed at her bottom lip, deep in thought, not seeing the looks exchanged between the three men. She looked up, a frown on her face. "Benen?"

"We'll get the basics for them. Then, you and your Mom can go shopping."

Chapter 21

Benen paced the conference room the next morning, his hands dug into his jeans pockets, his thoughts miles away. Some of the other men were already there, and he vaguely heard conversation and laughter around him. He finally paused behind the chair he had chosen, not wanting to sit until Cadee showed up, not really wanting to get the meeting underway, but he knew they needed to. They needed to heard what her parents had to say. That, he knew, would likely change everything. That scared him. He feared for Cadee's life.

He turned as he heard his name called and Ted walked towards him.

"Benen? We can't thank you enough for getting Cadee out when you did." Ted was agitated and Benen tilted his head, a frown on his face.

"Ted?"

Ted shook his head. "Cadee doesn't know yet, but the home we had down there was burned down the night after you two left."

Benen froze, his eyes on Ted, hearing the noise of conversation die away around him. "It was?" He rubbed at his head. "Then, if we hadn't left, we may not be here. Is that what you're saying?"

Ted shrugged. "It's impossible to know. A friend is quietly looking into it." He paused, his head turning to where he heard the women's voices approaching the room. "There's more. Dear Lord, I can't share it with Cadee, but I must. He's the only One who can truly protect her."

Cadee slipped into the chair Benen pulled out for her, suddenly shy. They had had words the night before and she knew she had to apologize to him. He had told her to take the bed, he would sleep in his office on the couch. She had protested, her hands folding the sweater he had picked out for her, placing it in one spot before she picked it up and repeated the process.

Benen had stood, his heart breaking for his bride, a prayer in it as well for patience, before he shoved away from the door he was leaning on and reaching to take her hands, stilling the movement, telling her it was okay, he had slept there before. It would be for one night, and he was fine with that. He had hugged her, dropped a kiss on the top of her head, murmured a prayer, and then walking to the door, opened it, hesitated a moment, before he walked out of the room, closing the door softly behind him. She didn't know that he had stood for moments outside the room, a prayer lifting to heaven before he could not longer utter any words, knowing that God understood his heart.

Benen scooted his chair into the table, his hand reaching for Cadee's, feeling the chilliness on it, and turned his head to watch her face. She's scared, Lord, and I don't want that for her. I want her at peace and happy. Please, dear Lord? Can we solve this and soon?

Barnabas looked around at the thirteen of his men sitting there, stern, sober looks on their faces before he looked at Ted and Mary, seeing the fatigue and worry and strain on their faces. His eyes then moved to Cadee and stopped, a frown appearing on his face. She was lost in thought and he needed her attention. He sighed. She was not an easy person to read, after all, and he would need to rely on Benen for that.

He cleared his throat, bringing all eyes to him, before he looked at Ted.

"Ted? Will you open our time of prayer? When we gather like this, we spend time in prayer, praying for one another and then the situation we find. Now that two of our men are married, their wives have become part of that prayer time." He smiled briefly at Cadee as she looked at him, wonder on her face, her mouth rounded as she took in what he said.

"That I will, Barnabas. I count it a privilege to do so." He looked around at the men, whose attention was focused on him. "You have all been prayed for over the many years that I have known of you. " He bowed his head, his throat working as he controlled his emotions, before his mouth opened and he prayed.

Barnabas finally raised his head, his eyes once more on Cadee, before moving to Benen and then her parents, knowing that when Ted spoke, everything changed. He shared a look with Breck, who had been researching the Daniells, finding something in their past that needed to be addressed and he wasn't quite sure how to do that. He needed to talk to Benen alone first. Breck nodded, knowing that Barnabas had made his decision about that.

"Ted?" Barnabas turned to him, finding Ted studying him closely. "We need to hear your story."

"That you do. And to do that, I think we'll need to go back a few years. Something happened a number of years ago that I am just now realizing does have an impact on what we faced." He turned to Cadee. "I'm so sorry, Cadee. If I had known back then what I know now, your life today would be different."

Cadee stared at her father, her mouth opening and closing. "Dad? What are you talking about?"

He sighed, reaching for Mary's hand, feeling hers tighten on his, aware that she knew just what he was talking about.

"It's like this, Cadee. God help us, we never meant to keep it a secret." His head bowed, Mary's arm around him.

"Mom? Dad? You're scaring me! What are you talking about?" Cadee's voice rose in fear, Benen's arm around her the only thing keeping her in her place. "Benen? Do you know?"

He shook his head. "No, Cadee darling. I don't." He watched with concern as Ted struggled to control his emotions.

"It's like this, Cadee." Ted looked at his daughter, sorrow on his face. "You're not our own. We adopted you when you were a week old. We should have told you years ago but we kept putting it off. Now, we have to bear the consequences of that."

There was dead silence in the room at his confession, the men exchanging glances, Breck's eyes on Benen, sorrow in them for his friend and his bride.

Cadee's head began to shake and they could see the dismay, distress, confusion on her face before she was on her feet running from the room, Benen on her heels, trying to catch up to her. Ted rose, staring after them, Mary's hand on his arm keeping him in place.

Buckley was on his feet as was Brady, following the two, knowing they were not safe. They searched for the two, finding Benen standing in the parking lot, staring around.

"Benen? Where's Cadee?" Brady slid to a stop, Buckley heading away from them.

"I have no idea. She was ahead of me and then just disappeared." Benen spun in a circle, not sure where she had got to. "She can't be far, but I need to find her."

The two men spun as they heard the roaring of a motor, Benen shoving Brady to one side as the van clipped him, sending him flying towards a snowbank that he landed awkwardly in, before laying still. The van doors flew open and men approached both Benen and Brady, weapons pointing at them. Brady's hands raised and then he was roughly shoved into the van, watching helplessly as Benen was dragged to the van and dumped into it, the men following, doors slamming shut as the van sped away, leaving the men who had ran for the outside staring in dismay after it.

Chapter 22

Barnabas ran for his vehicle, Brandon beside him, calling orders to the other men, who scattered, some to stay with Ted and Mary, the others to search for Cadee and Buckley. He shoved the truck into gear and sped away, searching desperately for the van, finally slowing as he reached town.

"I don't see it, Brandon. It couldn't have gotten that much of a start on us." His head swivelled as he searched.

"It didn't. They took a side road, likely the first one near our place. They would have been out of sight before we even hit the main road." Brandon turned in his seat, looking behind them before he pulled out his phone and made the call he didn't want to make. He pocketed his phone when he was finished. "There are officers responding."

"Good. Let's go back to that road and see if we can figure out which way they took. Were either of the men hurt, do you know?"

"I think Benen. I saw him shove Brady to one side before he was clipped by the van. The van blocked my view after that." His closed fist hit the door. "How did they know? How did they know they would come out at that particular time?"

"They've been watching. The security people said there have been different vehicles driving around the place on the roads. Not one that they can pinpoint as to being a problem." Barnabas' fingers on his left hand tapped at the wheel even as his eyes kept moving, desperate to find the van. "I have no idea where Cadee disappeared to. Do you?"

Brandon shook his head. "I don't. I would suspect Buckley went after her when Brady went after Benen."

Shutting his door carefully, Barnabas studied the activity going on, waiting at Breck approached.

"Breck? Any word?"

Breck shook his head. "Buckley found Cadee and she's in your office. We've kept her separate from her parents. Anna has a place ready for them, and they've agreed to move there. I'm sending Berneen and Baird in to shop for them as soon as we've been cleared to some extent." He looked around, the activity disturbing to him. "Any sign of our guys?"

"Not a one. We think they took the first road but with all the traffic that has come in since then, we can't get a sense of which way they turned." Barnabas walked towards the police chief who had responded.

"Will?" Barnabas' hand was out to shake the older mans, a friend of his father.

Will Peters shook his head. "Barnabas, what happened? You and I spoke last night. I would not have thought this could happen."

"There was a development this morning that shook Cadee's world and she ran, Benen after her. She was told she had been adopted at one week of age and she never knew this."

Will stared at him, his eyes narrowing. "And this just opens up a new game, doesn't it?" He shook his head. "We'll need to talk to her parents, as well as to her."

"We've Cadee in my office. Would you talk to her?"

"I can do that. Her parents?"

"Anna's put them into the guest suite on the main floor for now. I'm not sure how long they'll stay, given this. They have caused a whole lot of hurt to a young lady I cherish as a friend."

"They have." Will turned to walk with Barnabas towards the building. "Were either of your men hurt?"

"We think Benen. Brandon said he saw him clipped by the van but we can't be sure of that."

Will nodded, his hand on the door to open it. "Is there someone who can be with Cadee?"

"Berneen and Baird are. Anna is looking after her parents. Amy's away today - she had planned a trip with her husband." Barnabas hesitated at the office door, his hand on the handle. "Will, we need to activate the prayer chain."

"Already done. I called Jace first thing."

"Thanks." He still hesitated before he opened the door, walking into his office, hearing soft voices from his office, stopping as he saw Cadee almost running his way, his arms coming out to hug her.

"Barnabas?" Her voice was full of emotion as was the face she tilted back to him.

An arm around her, he turned her back to the office. "No word. It's too soon. We're looking, Cadee. We'll find him for you."

She nodded even as she sat back down into her chair, her hands rubbing along her jeans. "I know you'll do your best."

"We'll do more than our best." He perched on the corner of his desk, glancing quickly at Berneen and Baird. "Will Peters is the police chief of our town, Cadee. He needs to talk to you."

She nodded, not taking her eyes from Barnabas. "Mom and Dad?" She dropped her face to her hands. "How do I call them that, given what they have hidden?"

"They're still your parents, who love you deeply, Cadee. They didn't make the decision lightly not to tell you. There has to be a reason they didn't."

"I know, but that doesn't find Benen, does it?" She rose and was gone once more before they could stop her.

Berneen was on her feet, running after her friend, finding her standing in the lobby. Her arm around her, she drew her to the elevator.

"Come, Cadee. Come to our place. Baird will find us." She looked over her shoulder to see Baird and Barnabas standing there, Will behind them. "You need to get out of here. It's too open."

Cadee stopped, bringing Berneen to a halt as well. "No, I need to talk to them. I can't keep running. This doesn't solve anything." She turned, finding the men behind her. "Oh!"

"Berneen's right, Cadee." Baird spoke. "We'll go up to our place. That way, Berneen will feed us. We all need to eat."

Cadee shook her head. "I can't."

"You need to, Cadee." Will spoke up, years of experience behind his words. "I think Benen would want you to. Even just some soup."

She finally nodded, her hands reaching out to help Berneen, her mind not on what she was doing. Her thoughts drifted to what her parents and said, and her movements stopped, knowing she needed to confront them, but unwilling to do so without Benen. He was her support, her life, she thought. She needed him here with her, now.

Chapter 23

Cadee's thoughts drifted, the hum of conversation and activity around her fading as she returned to a few hours previously.

She had awakened that morning, was it only that morning, she thought, her arms wrapped around Benen's pillow. She shoved back her hair, and sat up, staring around the room, not sure where she was for a moment before she quickly slipped in for a shower and dressed rapidly, knowing Benen would need the room. She had quietly made her way to the kitchen, Benen soon there to help her.

They had eaten, she remembered, with not much conversation between then, her father shooting her glances she couldn't understand. They had walked down together to the conference room, she and her parents, finding seats before Barnabas started the meeting.

She couldn't remember now what she had said as her parents had told her that she was adopted. She had sprung from her chair, running from the room, shock on her face, sorrow deep in her heart. She heard Benen calling for her and had dodged out the door and around the side of the building, taking the walk that led to the garden area. She had hidden, her face covered with her arms as she waited, knowing he would find her, not willing to look up around. She had heard the squealing of tires and then shouts from the men before she heard another vehicle leave. She crouched down even further before she jumped, feeling a hand on her arm, raising her to her feet.

She looked up, afraid, the fear dissipating as she saw Buckley, his face grim as he studied her before his head turned towards the commotion they could both hear. He hustled her into a back door and then to Barnabas' office, shoving open the door and then seating her into a chair in the office itself, leaving and returning with a bottle of water he commanded her to drink.

She had glared at him, seeing the amusement lurking in his eyes before she had drank, not hearing the quiet footsteps that had approached the door, just seeing Buckley step away for a moment before she was on her feet, facing the door, seeing Baird and Berneen there, speaking quietly with Buckley before Berneen approached her.

"Cadee? You're okay?" Berneen reached to hug her, before she stood back, searching her face.

"No, I don't think I am. Where's Benen?" Her eyes flickered between the three of them before her head began to shake. "No! Where is he?"

"We don't know, Cadee. That noise you heard? He and Brady disappeared into a van and then the van disappeared. We're looking for them."

She shook her head, sinking back into her chair, her hand out to feel for the arm, eyes huge with fear.

"No, it can't be. He's here. He'll be here. I know he's here somewhere."

Buckley crouched down beside her, his hand on hers to still the motion. "I'm sorry, Cadee. He's not."

"He's not?" Her voice was broken, low, as she responded, seeing his head shaking. "Where is he?"

"We don't know. The guys are searching. The police are here."

"It's their fault."

"Whose?" Baird took the seat beside her, his eyes on her face, a frown in place.

"My parents. Or the couple that says they are." She slumped back in her seat, her hands rubbing at her face, tears she refused to shed shining in her eyes. "They did this."

"I don't know if they did, Cadee, but we'll talk with them. Bradon was making that his task. Do you want them to come here?"

She shook her head. "No, not right now. I need to sort through my thoughts, and I can't. Not with Benen missing." She was on her feet, pacing before she spun, her eyes on Buckley. "Buckley, what does God say?"

"That He loves you dearly. That He is here, no matter what you are facing. That He will protect Benen and Brady. That He knows what you are going through and is there, each step of the way. He has promised never to leave you, never to forsake you, to hide you in the hollow of His hand and cover you there."

She had listened soberly, her body relaxing as she heard his words. "He is. He is here." Her voice was very low, low enough the ones with her had to strain to hear them. "And he's with Benen. With Brady." She returned to her chair, reaching for the bottle of water, stopping to frown at it. "Berneen, there's something about a water bottle that I need to remember and I can't. What is it?"

Baird's hand was there, taking the bottle from her. "It will come. Let it rest. God will recall it to your memory when you need it. How about a cup of tea instead?"

"Do you have any juice, do you think? Orange juice sounds good." She sank back, her eyes closing, her face white, dark shadows under her eyes. She had not yet fully recovered from her poisoning and today she felt old, ancient, beyond a count of years. Her body ached as did her heart. Her head was pounding and she jumped as she felt a hand touch her. Her eyes opened, to find Berneen in Baird's chair, painkillers in her open hand. She stared at them before she took them, knowing she couldn't fight the headache or the pain wafting through her on her own.

Barnabas crouched down beside her, speaking to her. She looked around, finally just overcome with it all and just ran, stopping in the lobby, afraid to go outside, afraid to go back, just afraid. Too afraid to even pray.

Chapter 24

Cadee finally came back to the room she was in, her mind telling her it was time to pay attention to the conversation around her. She looked down at the table where she was sitting and the empty bowl in front of her. She had not even been aware that she had eaten. She sighed, the sigh welling from deep within her, not allowed to vocalize.

Barnabas had been watching her, knowing that she was sorrowing in more than one way, but not knowing how to help her. That frustrated him.

Berneen rested her arm around Cadee. "Cadee? You did eat some soup, but do you want anything more?"

Cadee shook her head, finally raising it to look for Barnabas, finding him sitting beside her.

He grinned at her momentary look of discomfort. "Didn't know I was that close?" He laughed and the sobered. "We do need to talk, Cadee. Will wants to go over what they're doing to find Benen and Brady."

She looked across the table at Will, finding his kindly eyes on her. "I'm sorry. I wasn't nice to you before."

Will shrugged. "I've had way worse. Don't worry about it. But Barnabas is right. We do need to talk." He shoved aside his plate, reaching for his cup and drinking from it before he put it back down, his hands cradling it. "Cadee, we are doing our best to find them. I have patrol officers scouring the surrounding neighbour, going door to door, working their way out in an ever increasing circle. We will find them, make no doubt about that."

"Will they be alive?" Her words were barely above a whisper.

Will shrugged. "We pray they are. It would be my guess they will be. Benen was taken for a reason and that reason seems to be you. Brady is incidental to that." He shared a look with Barnabas. "It is my guess that whoever was with him would have been taken. The good thing is that Brady is a paramedic, that if Benen is hurt, he can treat him as best he can."

"Are they together? You are sure of that?" Cadee voiced the question they all had been hesitant to.

"We have no reason to think they're not. In fact, I would suspect they will keep them together and use one against the other." Will smiled grimly as her face paled at his words. "I will not mince words with you, Cadee. I understand you like to be told what's going on. I would feel the same in your case."

She nodded, a frown on her face. "Why did they taken Benen? I was out there and hidden until Buckley found me."

"We know that. We think he was taken to use against you." Will watched as she swayed, Berneen's arm around her. "That's how they seem to be working." He looked up as he heard a tap at the door and then excused himself as Baird reappeared, beckoning for him.

———

115

Cadee looked around, knowing she was surrounded by friends, something she had missed for so many years, not having them down where her parents had served.

"Barnabas, what about the mission?"

"What about it?" His voice was quiet, controlled, not showing the anger he was feeling, anger he would need to deal with. Right now, his focus was on the young woman sitting beside him, and finding both Benen and Brady.

"The mission. Was it ever legitimate?" She heard the others gasp at her words but not Barnabas. "It wasn't, was it?"

"Our Foundation researched it before we became supporters. It was up until about two months ago, about the time your father received that letter. From what we can understand, it was taken over, a hostile takeover if you want to term it that way. The other missionaries out with it were told to come home, the mission was closing. Supporters were notified. We only received notification this past week. They delayed it, knowing we would launch a full investigation, which we have done. Breck is working on that, and he's not happy, to say the least, with what he's finding."

She nodded. "And you need to talk with Dad and Mom." She paused, biting at her lip, fighting back tears. "This has been a horrible day. How do I talk to them?"

Barnabas shook his head. "None of us can tell you that. We will pray with you. We will pray with them. Buckley is willing to sit in as your pastor, if you want. Anna and Doc have both come to me, saying they want to be there. Doc in particular is concerned as you have never fully healed yet from what you went through. If it helps, any one of us will be there. All of us if that's what you want. Berneen has specifically asked to sit with you."

Cadee's eyes searched the faces in the room, seeing only love and concern, not the condemnation she expected to see. She finally nodded.

"Tomorrow? I can't today." She shoved back from the table and walked away. They heard the outside door open and close.

Berneen was on her feet, following, watching as Cadee stood outside their apartment door, her hand on the knob before she twisted it and walked in, shutting out her friend and shutting out the world.

Cadee slowly slid down the door to sit in a crumpled heap against it, tears she didn't know she was shedding on her face, before she was on her feet, running for the bedroom, throwing herself down on the bed, her arms wrapping around Benen's robe that he had thrown carelessly on it that morning, sobs finally shaking her body. Her sobs spent, she slept. Unable even to pray, her sobs wafted to God as those very   prayers

Rousing slowly the next morning, Cadee raised her head, not aware of where she was for a moment. Her arms tightened for a moment on Benen's robe before she set it aside and rose, heading for a shower, finding clean clothes and then making her way to the kitchen. She stood, fridge door open, not wanting to eat, but knowing that she had to. Squinting as she looked at the clock, she sighed. It was late, later than she thought.

She turned as she heard a tap at the door and cautiously made her way to it, peeking through the pinhole, before she stepped back, pulling the door open, letting Berneen and Anna enter.

Anna took one look at her young friend and simply swept her into a hug, holding her as she shuddered with her intense emotions. Berneen stood, her hand rubbing Cadee's back before she moved away, heading for the kitchen.

"Have you eaten yet, Cadee?"

Cadee turned at Berneen's words. "No. I just got up. I never sleep this late." She yawned as she slumped down into a chair, watching as Anna reached for the tea kettle and the tea and Berneen reached for bread.

"French toast coming up. We haven't eaten either."

Conversation was quiet among the three women as they ate. Cadee finally rose as she heard a knock at the door, stepping back to let Barnabas and Bradon enter, pointing to the kitchen.

"There's coffee. I made it without thinking." She slid into her chair, staring down at her unfinished breakfast before she pushed it away. "Barnabas? Why are you here?"

He grinned at her from his seat on the other side of the table. "Direct and to the point. I like that about you, Cadee." His smile faded as he sipped at his coffee. "Have you see your parents since yesterday?"

She shook her head. "No. I need to. Why?"

"Because they're not here." Shocked silence followed his words.

"They're gone?" Cadee sat back, thinking through the few hours she had spent with them. "That wasn't them. They would have had baggage with them. There was something off about them all along." She raised her eyes to Barnabas and Bradon. "Imposters? What did they leave here in the apartment?"

"That's what we need to find out. We're moving you out of here for now until Brandon can do a sweep. Bradon will bring Kade through as well." He looked down at their dishes. "Just leave everything for now. Grab what you need - your purse, Bible, clothes."

She stared at him for a moment, before she was on her feet, running for the bedroom. They could hear drawers opening and closing, the sound of hangers hitting the floor, and then her hurried footsteps to the office, before she appeared in the kitchen doorway, a bag in her hand, her jacket on, sneakers on her feet.

"Where am I to go?"

Barnabas held up a hand and simply pointed to the door. They followed him out and then down to his office, Bradon staying in the apartment.

He spoke on the phone for a while before he turned to Cadee. "Cadee?" He slipped into the chair beside her, not moving behind his desk. "Security shows the couple leaving about two this morning. They walked out to the road where a car was waiting for them. We don't have enough information on that car to track it."

She nodded. "It just didn't seem like them. They looked like them, sort of sounded like them, but there was something off."

"What do you mean?"

"Just the way they spoke. It was as if they were playing a part, with a dialogue they had been given." She looked up at them. "Dad would have wanted to pray first, and that man didn't. He just ignored that." She studied Barnabas. "You don't know him, so you wouldn't have known." Her eyes slid shut. "That's why."

"Why what, Cadee?" When she didn't respond, Barnabas shared a look with the other two women and then with Breck who had entered silently, closing the door behind him and leaning on it.

———

120

"Benen. That's why he was taken. He would have known. I think he did. I could see him watching them closely, a puzzled look on his face."

Barnabas nodded. "That's the conclusion we've come to. Our guys are out there searching, they've taken leave from their employment for now."

"They can't do that!" Cadee was horrified.

"They can and will. I think we've talked about this, but The Foundation pays them. That means I can call on them when I need their help. Their employers are all hand picked by The Foundation and in agreement with this."

She finally nodded herself. "I remember." Her voice was low. "What about your volunteer activities?"

"They know as well. Right now, we are searching. They can't have been taken too far away. That's a given. They need to watch you. You have been shaken by what you were told. We need to work through that, and we will. Right now, we need to get you settled into a new place."

"Here?" Cadee had no hope that it would be and that Benen would never find her

Barnabas nodded again. "It is. There is a small suite beside Doc and Anna's and next to mine. We'll put you there. It's one that has full security in it. We've needed it before and likely will again. For now, it's yours and Benen's, until we find whoever it is that is after you."

She reached to hug him before she rose, Anna's arm around her, before Barnabas stopped her.

"Your things? Did you notice anything odd about them?"

She shook her head. "No. Should I have?"

Barnabas thought for a moment. "Have Anna look at them. She knows what to look for. Who would suspect her of finding something? Anna, the other office here before you go up."

Chapter 26

Two days later, Cadee rose, walking through the small suite. It was smaller than Benen's she knew, with just one bedroom and other rooms. She sighed. She wanted Benen home but then she would have to face her growing feelings for him and right now, that was something she was so unsure of.

She thought of her parents, praying they were still alive, and safe. *Lord, protect them, please? I need them. Benen needs them. I feel so bad for Brenden and Brandon. They feel guilty but they would not have known. There is just no way. I think they planned on that, whoever they is.*

She paused in the kitchen, her hands automatically reaching to make a cup of tea, her eyes on the window over the sink. She finally turned as she heard a tap at her door, moving that way slowly, feeling beaten up and beaten down.

Baird watched her closely as she moved around the kitchen, not really thinking of what she was doing, before she set a mug of coffee in front of him and pushed over the open cookie jar.

"Anna left some cookies. I am sure they are delicious. I just haven't had an appetite to try them."

"That's understandable." He sipped at his coffee before he replaced his mug on the table and folded his hands. "Cadee, I'm not here by chance. Barnabas asked me to be here with you. Berneen would be but she had a commitment she couldn't get out of. She'll be by later."

She studied him, her eyes narrowing. "This sounds like an all-day babysitting job."

He laughed at her nonsense. "I guess you could say that. Barnabas has to be away with some of the men. The others are here on site."

"And why would he be away?" Hope flared in her eyes. "They've found them?"

"We have a lead on where they may be. Barnabas is going in, taking Bradon and Kade for one, to see if they can really spot them or if it's another false lead. We have been swamped with those as have the police."

"But will that be okay with the police?"

Baird nodded. "Will has gone with them. He said he could do nothing other than that." He paused, gathering his thoughts. "They don't know when they'll be back. Barnabas was hoping by early afternoon, but it depends on what they find."

"I get that." She rubbed at the table, wiping away an imaginary spot. "About that couple?"

"Yes, that couple. Breck has found that they are connected to the takeover of the mission. How he did that, I have no idea, but he found that out. He stated to me that he still had a lot of research to do, but that somehow that couple is connected to your parents. He's shown their photo to some of the other missionaries, ones who know your family. They are adamant that couple are imposters. They have given us some leads to follow to find your parents. One of them has heard from your Dad. They are in the States, making their way slowly this way.”

“They’re alive?” Cadee’s face lit up with joy, hope, and relief. “Oh, thank God. I was so afraid they were dead and buried somewhere I would never find them.” She sobered. “Did they leave anything in Benen’s?”

“They did. I can’t tell you what as the police have now become involved, but yeah, they did. Some of it was done right dangerous. Food stuff that could have killed either one of you. I think that was the plan. Somehow, they are using you and also Benen to try and get at your Dad. That we need to talk to your Dad about.”

Baird and Berneen finally left late that evening, leaving Cadee to lock up after them, and then wander the suite, her arms wrapped around herself, not wanting to retire but not wanting to stay up. She was on edge, Baird’s words to her earlier puzzling her. What did they want from Dad? And who are they, anyway? Do I know them?

She finally sighed, headed for the bedroom, and then ready for bed, sat for the longest time on the side of her bed, not thinking, not praying, not sure what she should be doing or thinking. She finally looked up, breathing a prayer that was inaudible but knowing God read her heart and understood her unspoken words, hopes and dreams.

She slept, not hearing the lock click open and closed and then the quiet footsteps heading her way. She didn’t see the tall familiar form that stood staring down at her before he too headed for a shower.

Benen stood once more staring down at her before he crawled in beside her, wrapping his bride in his arms, tears wetting her hair, his words too inaudible to any one but God.

Chapter 27

Rousing early the next morning, Cadee felt disoriented for a few moments. She laid still, her senses warning her she was not alone. She slowly opened her eyes, staring at the wall in front on her before she shifted her body, feeling weight on her abdomen. Afraid, she twisted even more, her face coming close to Benen's as he slept, his body totally relaxed in his fatigue and weariness, his arm anchoring her to him. Her eyes grew round, and she struggled to free an arm, her hand coming up to touch his face before tears clouded her eyes and she wept, her heart raising in praise that he was back. She wiped at her eyes, taking in his face, the changes she could see that hurt her.

She laid back, her hand locked around his arm before she slowly shifted away from him and stood, her eyes on him, then rushing to find her clothes, the bathroom door clicking softly behind her. Once dressed, she stood again, her eyes taking in his face before she stooped, a gentle kiss on his cheek, and then she headed for the kitchen, her eyes squinting at the time. Just after seven. She reached for her phone, hesitating for a moment before she dialled.

A rough voice answered. "Hello?"

"Barnabas?" She was hesitant, it didn't sound like him. "I'm sorry. I woke you up."

"It's okay, Cadee. Are you all right?" She could hear him shifting around.

"What time did you get back?"

"Around midnight. That's after we had them checked out at Emerge. They're okay, Doc said. Tired. Beaten up a bit. Need some food." Barnabas' voice didn't tell everything, and that she knew. She would have to wait.

"Thank you." She set down her phone, staring at it, then spinning in a circle. Anna had made sure to stock their kitchen with essentials as she called them. Cadee stood back in the kitchen doorway, her eyes on the bedroom before her feet took her back that way, finding Benen had arisen as well, the sound of the shower coming to her ears.

She turned once more to the kitchen, knowing she needed to feed him, just not what. She finally pulled out food, set his coffee, made her tea, and then waited, her arms folded around herself, her eyes staring out the kitchen window. Lost in thought, she didn't hear Benen approaching the kitchen door, stopping as he saw her there, waiting for him, before he was across the room, enfolding her in his arms, his tears wetting her hair.

She spun, her arms round him as sobs shook her body. They finally stood back from one another, his hands on her arms, studying her face.

"Benen? How?"

"God. That's the only way they found us. We were hidden quite well. Somehow, Kade picked up the slightly scent and followed it, finding us yesterday afternoon. It took them a while to reach to us where we were. And no, they didn't find the men responsible." He shook his head at her. "Will, the police chief, will be by later today, he said. They took our statements yesterday but he wants to talk to us both."

She nodded, before pointing to a chair. "You need to eat. We can talk later." When he didn't release her, she looked up, a puzzled look on her face. "Benen?"

He simply cupped her cheek, bent and kissed her, a lingering kiss that neither wanted to end.

She stood, her eyes on him when he stepped back, not sure what had happened, only knowing her heart had warmed.

"Benen?"

He turned, a smile just for her on his face, and spoke. "Cadee, my darling. I missed you. We'll talk, my darling. But first, you've told me I need to eat."

She stared at him, her mouth dropping open until he winked, and then she laughed.

"Benen! Only you!"

Barnabas studied the two of them later than morning, even as he set his mug down on his desk, and pointed to the chairs near the couch in his office. He reached for a folder, knowing he needed to break some bad news to Cadee, but not willing to just yet. He looked up as Will entered followed by Brandon. He nodded at Will, knowing Will likely had details to hash out with Benen.

Cadee looked up at that point, her face paling at the grim looks on the men's faces, her hands reaching for   Benen's.

Benen looked between the three men and sighed. He was still feeling not himself and that he knew would be a while. He reached to wrap an arm around Cadee, pulling her close to him. Barnabas had told him the night before how they had had to move Cadee from his apartment, that Brandon and the police had gone through it, finding dangerous objects planted there. He had stared at Barnabas before he questioned him, learning that the couple was not Cadee's parents after all.

Cadee broke the silence. "Will?"

"Cadee? We have some news. Some good news. Some bad news."

"Good news first, please and thank you. I can use all the good news I can get."

Will laughed at her, the sound breaking the solemnity of the moment. "Well, you will like this. We have found your parents. The real ones, this time. A friend on a force in the States found them at a homeless shelter. I understand Andy is on his way down with Breck to bring them home for you."

She stared at him. "Mom? Dad? You found them? Oh, thank God!"

Will smiled. "That we have. Andy told me they'll likely wait until tomorrow to come back. My friend wants to talk to them, to find out what they can tell them. He said what you're going through sounds too familiar to him."

"You mean, another mission?"

Will nodded. "That's correct. He didn't give a lot of information, so I don't have much to share with you." He looked over at Benen. "Now, for the bad news."

"There's always that, isn't there?" They laughed at Cadee's quiet muttering.

"The couple who were here? They were found. Unfortunately, we'll not be able to speak with them. Their bodies washed up on the lakeshore a few miles from here."

Cadee paled. "Murdered! How cruel!"

"It is cruel, Cadee, but they would have known that would likely be their fate, if they had really thought about it." Brandon spoke this time. "The research we've been doing shows us that it is a very vicious, vindictive, cruel, evil man behind all this. We don't have the evidence we need at this point to arrest him."

Cadee had been watching him closely, her hand gripping Benen's tightly before she sighed. "House arrest! I just know it! We're not going to have any freedom, are we?"

They laughed at her grumbling and at her smirk, knowing she had done that on purpose.

"Seriously, Cadee. It will seem like that, but we'll let you have as much freedom as we can let you have. Benen can work from his office here as much as he can. Now you, what are we to do with you?"

———

131

Barnabas shook a finger at you. "Doc tells me you're not well enough yet to work. So, tell us. What do you want to do in the meantime?"

She shrugged. "All I know is the work from the mission office. I mean, I did study at college, getting my diploma in music, but I have no idea what to do with that. I never did. I'm not sure why I took that."

Benen watched her closely, knowing she was reluctant to say what she had played. "She plays the violin and viola, Barnabas."

Barnabas sat back, wonder on his face, before he turned to Will. "Will?"

Will was nodding. "Just who we need. Cadee, we'll like to ask something of you, but feel free to say no. Our youth are putting on a concert this Sunday night. We had a violinist booked but he fell ill and is unable to make it. We can manage without one but if you would be willing, we'd appreciate it."

She stared at him, then turned to Benen, finding him watching her closely, knowing without being told he would back whatever decision she made. "I don't know, Will. I have no instrument. Mine disappeared about six weeks ago. We found it shattered in our garden. We have no idea who did that."

Will shared a long look with the other men before he spoke. "Jace."

Barnabas was nodding. "Jace. He'll help."

"Jace? I'm sorry, I don't understand."

"Jace has a music store, Cadee. If he doesn't have an instrument to suit, he will track one down within hours." Benen hugged her tighter. "It's your choice, my darling. We will do what you want."

She sighed, knowing she missed her music. "I would need to see the instrument. But first, what about Benen? Where did you find him?"

Benen's hug tightened even more as he watched her face. "We were about three miles from her, Cadee. Kade found us. It's not going to be easy for you to hear, that much I know."

She nodded, her eyes searching the faces of the men. "I didn't think it would be pretty or easy to hear, but I need to. It's my fault, somehow, that you and Brady were taken."

"That's the interesting part, Cadee. We're not so sure on that any more." Barnabas' words had her eyes on him, puzzlement on her face.

Chapter 29

Cadee rose, heading for the coffee pot and refilling their mugs, the kettle whistling softly until she unplugged it and made her tea. She glanced at the clock. Lunchtime, but who felt like eating?

She slid down beside Benen again, feeling his arm around her, her eyes on Barnabas, then Will, and then Brandon.

"Who talks first?"

Barnabas just shook his head. He was beginning to understand Cadee, to some degree, to know how she covered her feelings. This was one way, going on the offensive.

"I will, I guess." Barnabas sipped at his coffee, before sitting back, his mug cradled in his hands. "I have to take you back to the day it happened. You know how we tried to find them. We had suspicions all along that they had simply taken the first road and then disappeared on it. That is exactly what happened. Will's patrol officers finally found the car two days ago, hidden in an abandoned barn."

"Is that the one that's near the lake?" Cadee spoke up. "I saw it one day and wondered about it."

"That's the one." Will took over the conversation. "We had to search a large area around that barn. Kade picked up the scent of one of them and took off, Bradon after him. We lost them for a while but eventually connected. The men were in the basement of an abandoned, collapsed house. Sheltered from the weather for the most part. For some reason, the place was warmer than outside and it shouldn't have been."

"God." Cadee breathed only one word. "God provided and protected."

"That He did, Cadee." Brandon took over now. "We had to crawl to the back of the basement and there was only room for two of us to go in. We found Benen and Brady with their wrists fastened to the wall, unable to move very far. We were able to release them and then send them out one at a time, Burney going first, then Benen, Brady and lastly myself. We made it out and before we could more than move away, the building finished collapsing. It had only been held up by a few rafters as far as we could see and it appears our going in and out jostled them in some way."

Cadee had paled, her hand gripping Benen's. "Tell me you found some evidence."

They all shook their heads. "We didn't. The men who put them in there were very careful. Both Benen and Baird were unconscious at the time and can tell us nothing of how they were placed in there. We suspect the building wasn't as demolished as we found it. Will has a team going over it now to see what they can find."

Cadee paled even more before her face turned up to Benen. "You never said. How bad?"

"How bad?"

She nodded. "How bad were you hurt?"

He shrugged. "Knocked out. Bumps and bruises. Nothing that will not heal, Cadee." He looked up at Barnabas. "But you have news other than this."

Barnabas nodded, a sigh welling within him that he kept down. "I do and I'm not sure how to even tell you." He held out the folder, Benen hesitant to take it. "It seems as if your past has come back as well."

Benen frowned. "My past? I have no past."

Cadee was staring at him. "Benen? Didn't you say something about a grandfather or an uncle at some point? They were into smuggling."

Benen groaned, his eyes sliding shut. "Great uncle Benjamin. I had forgotten. There were rumours that he was into smuggling, particularly during the Thirties and the Depression, but nothing was ever proven. Dad said he always denied it, but he was never comfortable with that denial. Dad always felt there was a sliver of truth to it." His hand rubbed at his jeans leg, his eyes on the floor. "I don't know if I could ever deny it or prove it, Barnabas."

"Not at this point. But Breck did find some evidence of a link to the mission, a large sum of money given by your Grandmother. It appears it came from your Great uncle. She told the staff there that she had no idea where he got it. They mentioned something about proceeds from smuggling, having heard the rumours but she shook her head at them, according to what was recorded. She states he had received money from his wife's family and that was what they had been living on. When he died, he asked that she give it to someone who needed it. They had no children."

"No, they never did. Uncle Ben was a quiet man, never saying much. He could have been into smuggling or it could have come from his wife's family. How do we prove that as this point?"

"Breck is still looking into that, but he doesn't seem to think he can prove it either, it's been too long." Barnabas sat back, his eyes shifting between Cadee and Benen. "That's not all. The mission you were under, Cadee? I know we've talked about what happened. The board that was there have been let go. The mission is essentially closed. We are still looking into the men who did the takeover. Will seems to think it was done illegally and has asked a detective to investigate."

Will nodded. "It's too big an issue to let go, Cadee. I'm sure you, your parents, and everyone else, including the supporters and sponsors, want answers."

They finally rose, not much further ahead in what they knew or suspected. Cadee felt they were keeping things from her and resented that before she shook her head, knowing they had to. It was a police investigation after all.

Chapter 30

Cadee stood again in the kitchen of their suite, listening to Benen and Brandon talk, knowing they would soon head her way. She glanced at the clock, mid afternoon, she thought. None of them had had lunch, too busy talking to remember. She reached for the fridge, pulling open the door, and then closing it. She didn't feel like eating, her stomach in too many knots from what they had been told, and knowing how close it had been for Benen. She turned, a frown on her face. He had glossed over his time away from her too quickly. That was something she meant to ask him. She headed for the door as she heard a knock, pulling it open to find Brady standing there, his hand raised to knock again.

She stood for a moment before reaching to hug him and then pulling him into the suite, to the kitchen where she silently pointed to a chair before placing a mug of coffee in front of him, sliding into a chair opposite him, her eyes on him.

Brady frowned, and then smiled. "You want to know what happened?"

"I do. I was told about how they found you and what happened to that building." She shuddered at the thought. "But not what happened before then, after you were taken." She pointed at his chin. "You didn't have that bruise before that day."

He rubbed at it, a grimace on his face. "No, I didn't. Benen hasn't said anything?"

She shook her head. "We really haven't had a chance to talk, but there'll be things he doesn't know or doesn't remember. I need you to tell me it all, Brady. All."

He searched her face, a prayer for wisdom drawn from him, before he nodded. "Okay, then. It's not pretty."

"It never is. I have been around the block a few times, Brady. You have not seen what I have seen. But you're a paramedic. You'll understand, that I know."

"I gathered it wasn't the nicest of places you lived. And with the war on, that makes it even worse."

"It does." She shivered in remembrance, jumping as she felt a hand on her shoulder, looking up to find Benen sliding into the chair beside her. "Benen?"

"It's okay, my darling. I've been told. And I told them you would want to know, would demand to know in fact." He laughed as he ducked the elbow she aimed at him.

Brady grinned even as he shook his head at them. "Enough, you two. Let's behave."

"I always do. It's Benen that has trouble with that." Cadee smirked at Benen, hearing his protest that he had no trouble acting like an adult.

Brady shook his head once more before he sobered. "Benen, for a while there, I thought you were dead. You do know that?"

Benen nodded. "I remember you telling me that, but it's all so hazy, even getting out of there."

"Doc said you took more than one blow. The first one was when they hit you with the van and you were knocked out. The second one must have been when I was unconscious too."

"You were unconscious? Brady, what did they do to you two?" Cadee's horrified voice broke through the silence after Brady's words.

"That we don't know, Cadee. We'll have to ask them when we find them. And we will find them, trust me on that. Our guys are mad and you don't make them mad. They're a force to be reckoned with at any time, but when they're angry, look out world." Brady's thoughts drifted for a few moments before he looked back at Cadee.

"Cadee, to go back to the beginning. You had disappeared. I followed Benen, thinking to help him look for you. The van was there before either one of us saw it, coming in-between us and the building. Benen, you shoved me aside, I think, but didn't make it away in time. The doors flew open, they dragged you in and just dumped you on the metal floor. I was on my feet, ready to fight for you when they pointed a weapon at me and then forced me into the van. They wouldn't let me near you, and I fought them on that. That's when they knocked me down with the blow to the chin. I must have hit my head because I don't remember anything until we were being pulled from the van later that day. I don't know what they did to avoid being found. We were shoved through a woods to that building. I had to help you, you could barely put one foot in front of the other."

Chapter 31

Brady's mind slipped back to that day and the kitchen faded from his vision. He remembered the fear he felt as he had been forced into the van, seeing Benen sprawled face down, lifeless, he thought. He had demanded to tend to him, but had been prevented from getting to him. He had insisted, fighting the men in the back of the van until a blow to his chin sent him tumbling backwards, his head striking metal before he laid still himself.

He had aroused hours later, how many he wasn't sure, feeling himself being pulled from the van, reaching for Benen as he tumbled from the van, helping him to stand upright, his eyes on the masked men in front of him, protesting that Benen needed medical attention.

They were forced through the woods, stumbling over the hidden fallen branches and debris, brought to a halt in front of a ramshackle house, that had begun the process of falling in on itself. He shifted Benen's arm around his shoulders and his grip around Benen's back, waiting for what he had no idea.

They were forced to walk to the edge of the building, to an open area, when sudden movements on the part of the men sent first Benen, and then himself, tumbling over the edge and through a hole in the floor, to land awkwardly on the basement floor. He groaned, turning himself over and then reaching for Benen, finding men in his way, dragging him backwards to a wall. He fought them, trying to get free and to Benen. He knew his friend needed medical attention. Shoved roughly down, his head slamming back again the foundation, his vision darkened for a moment, before he aroused, feeling his wrists encased in something. He tugged at them, desperate to escape, hearing the hoarse laughter of the men before they were gone.

He tugged again, not able to get loose, searching for a way out. He finally looked at his wrists, first one and then the other, despair darkening his vision. Shackles held his arms to the wall, giving him little room to move them. His head went back again, as prayers poured from his heart.

Benen, he thought, his attention turning to his friend, finding him chained in a similar manner, his head down. I need to get to him. He's hurting, and I need to take care of him. He tugged harder at the shackles, not finding them giving way.

Night came and went as did the next day. Brady tried repeatedly to escape to no avail. The next night came and went. The men had appeared that evening, bring food and water, letting them rise for a few minutes before they were once more shackled to the wall. Brady despaired of ever getting away. He was concerned about Benen.

Then, he frowned. Nothing had been asked of them. They had not had to answer any questions. No photos had been taken with them holding that day's paper. So, why had they been taken? He knew he was incidental to Benen's captivity, in the wrong place at the wrong time, but it didn't make a lot of sense. He prayed that Cadee was safe, that his friends or the police would find them.

The next morning, he shivered slightly in the cooler air, being struck by the thought that they had not suffered from the cold. God, is that You? Protecting us? Thank you.

His eyes went to Benen, his head tilting as he studied him as best he could in the darkness, not able to see him very clearly.

"Benen?" There was no response, so he kicked lightly at Benen's foot, rousing him somewhat. "Benen? Come on. Wake up."

He heard Benen moving slightly before his raspy hoarse voice responded.

"Brady? What? Where are we?"

"Not at home, that's for certain. How are you feeling?" He waited, his mouth opening to repeat his words when Benen responded.

"I hurt. All over. Where are we? What happened?" Benen tugged at his wrists. "What are these things?"

"We're shackled to a wall, in a basement of that abandoned house near the lake. You know the one about five miles from home?"

"Oh, that one. Why? What time is it?"

"Better question would be what day. We've been here a good day and a half. You were knocked flying by a van, knocked out, thrown in the van. I tried to get you out, but was taken captive myself."

"That was real smart of you. It doesn't explain why." Benen's voice was fading.

"Stay with me, Benen. I need you to stay awake."

"Sorry, my head is aching and it's hard to keep my eyes open. Did you get a look at the guys that did this?" A hopeful note crept into Benen's voice.

"No, I didn't. They were wearing masks. Benen, do you have any idea why? Benen?" Brady sighed to himself. Benen had faded away on him again. He didn't like that. Benen needed medical attention and soon.

Hours passed, with Benen awake on and off. Brady tried to occupy his mind, running through all the verses he had memorized, spending time in prayer, thinking through the next few weeks and what he needed to accomplish. His head turned and he frowned during the late morning, hearing a sound.

He tensed, hearing the sound coming closer to him. Then a head appeared through the debris. His friends were there. Quietly they studied the shackles, finding a way to release them and then shoving the men forward through the area that they had just used.

Hands outside pulled Benen and Brady to their feet and hurried them away, intent on getting them to safety. Cracking and groaning behind them had them all spinning, watching in horror as the building settled even more.

"Thanks, guys. That was just in time." Brady shared a look with Barnabas before nodding at Benen. "He needs medical attention."

"And so do you."

Late that evening, into the early morning of the next day, Benen and Brady walked towards their building, surrounded by their friends and police officers Will had sent with them, their hearts grateful for their friends' determination not to stop until they were found. Words would never express their thanks, that much they knew.

Brady watched as Benen stumbled slightly as he climbed the stairs, refusing the elevator. He knew why. It would feel too confining. He himself wasn't sure he could ever enter an elevator again.

He returned to the present, to find Cadee's face filled with horror and shock, her body shaking with her emotions, her hand tight on Benen's before she rose and came and hugged him.

"Thank you, Brady. I can only imagine how hard it was for you." Her emotions getting the better of her, she turned and ran from the room, leaving Benen and Brady staring at one another, knowing that their lives would never be the same again, not after what they had been through.

Chapter 32

Two days later, Cadee stood in Jace's music shop, her eyes huge as she looked around, wandering the shop, studying the instruments there before she turned to Benen.

"Benen? I didn't know this store was here."

"I didn't have a chance to tell you. I knew I'd lose you if I did." He simply grinned at her pleasure, glad he could help with her time recovering. "Jace said he had a violin or a viola, whichever one you wanted to try." He nodded to the counter. "Over here."

Jace watched with pleasure as Cadee studied the two instruments, her hands gentle as she picked one up and then the other, finally taking the violin and tuning it, the bow tightened as well. Her eyes closing as she raised the violin to her shoulder, the bow was drawn across it, music poured from it, hymns of thankfulness filling the store. She played for a while, before setting it aside and reaching for the viola, repeating the steps she had just taken.

She looked up, her face happy, a smile on it. "Jace. These are wonderful instruments. Don't tell me you had these for sale."

"Actually, I do. They are part of an estate sale that I was asked to be part of. I have spoken with the family. They wish you to take both, at no charge."

"I can't do that."

"It's their wish, Cadee. All they want is for them to be used. It's their way of saying thank you for your service in the missions. That's what they've told me."

She turned to Benen, finding him shrugging. "Benen?"

He shrugged. "If it's what they want, Cadee, I don't see that you can say no."

She struggled with her answer, finally turning to Jace. "I guess I have to say thank you. I never expected this quality of instruments though."

"The previous owner played with an orchestra and travelled the world as a solo artist. They just wanted them loved and used." Jace laid a hand on hers. "You have a wonderful talent, Cadee. It would be a shame not to use it."

She nodded. "I was told they needed me for Sunday night. I haven't seen the music." She looked up at him as he laughed, then started to laugh herself. "You were that sure?" She reached for the music.

"No, I was that hopeful. We have prayed about this. God told us not to worry, that He would provide and He did. If you're not comfortable with this, we understand. Barnabas and Brandon have talked to us. We can set you up so you're not in sight. That had been the original wish of the violinist we booked, but the committee overruled him. We won't let them do that to you."

"Thank you. I would like to be out of sight. I think it would be much safer, given what we've been through."

"That it will, Cadee. Now, Jace, is there a practice coming up tonight or tomorrow night?"

"Tomorrow night. If Cadee can make it, we'd appreciate it. But again, no pressure. If you're not able to, that's fine."

Jace watched them walk away, not sure if Cadee would be there. She's got talent, Lord, talent she should be using. But it's Your timing, isn't it? Not ours. Protect this young couple.

Benen placed the instruments in the trunk, watching Cadee as she leaved through the music.

"Can you do it?" His quiet words broke into her thoughts.

She nodded. "I can. I just need to know it's safe for everyone if I do this. I don't want anyone hurt because of me."

"We get that, Cadee. We do. Barnabas and Will have assured me they will take care of that." He hugged her, then opened the car door. "Do you want to do some shopping while we're in town?"

She shrugged. "I guess I should. Christmas is almost here." She sighed. "How many do I buy for?"

"Only the ones you really want to."

She glared at him. "Then, that's everyone. Do you know that?"

He began to laugh. "I do, my darling. That I do. Who do you want to start with?"

"I need to find a good music store that sells CDs. Is there one in town?"

He laughed even harder, pointing to the shop they had just left. "Jace has the best selection in town."

She groaned, her hands covering her face. "How did I know you would say that?"

Chapter 33

Drawing a deep breath Sunday night, Cadee drew the bow across the violin for the first note. She had opted to bring both instruments, not sure which one she wanted to use. Benen sat near her, his eyes on her, just as he had many times in the past. She watched him for a moment, before she was caught up into the music, as always, and then forgot about where she was and who was around her. Barnabas stood where he could see her, but hidden from her view, surprise on his face. She's good, he thought, good enough to tour. Will she choose that, I wonder? Then his attention was drawn to those few around them, most of them his men or police officers in plain clothes, volunteers Will had told him. It didn't surprise him that there were so many.

Cadee finally put the instrument away, carefully packing it into its case, coming back to the present as Benen hugged her.

"You're better than you ever were."

"I just got lost in the music. I shouldn't have. That was dangerous." She looked around, not seeing the men and women who had been there.

"It's okay. Barnabas and Will looked out for you."

Barnabas stood for a moment watching her, before he spoke. "Cadee. Benen. Let's get you two home. We can go out the back door. Breck has the van there for us."

Cadee followed, not seeing the couple standing watching her, Brandon and Brenden beside them.

Ted spoke. "She has always had a talent for that instrument. She was devastated when hers was destroyed. We could never figure out why."

"That's part of what we're looking into. Come on, you two. Let's get you to your suite. Tomorrow is time enough to let Cadee know you're here."

Mary nodded. "I just don't know how she'll take it, given what she went through." She sighed, her hand reaching for Ted's as they watched the traffic from the back seat of the car. "How did they manage that?"

"That's something we don't know." Brenden turned to look at them. "They really did look and sound like you two. I think Cadee was hesitant, picking up on something, but not sure what. She did say you didn't protest at staying in Benen's apartment, not like she thought you would."

"And we would have, given they're newlyweds, no matter how or why they married. We wouldn't have intruded, but this other couple seemed to insist on that?"

Brandon's head flipped around before his eyes sought the road again, his hands tight on the wheel. "That's what puzzled me. They insisted they had to be with her."

Ted shared a look with Brenden. "How much did they do?"

Brenden sighed, knowing he would have to tell them. "They left a lot of dangerous items and materials planted throughout the apartment. With Cadee running like she did and Benen disappearing, we moved Cadee to the secure suite we have. The couple left, Cadee not wanting to talk to them after them telling her she had been adopted at one week of age."

"They told her what?" Ted's voice hardened as he worked to control his emotions, Mary's hand tightening on his. "How cruel!"

"That's why she ran. With her running, Benen took off after her. That action of her saved both their lives. If she hadn't run, the police think some of the objects would have been triggered and Cadee and Benen killed."

Mary's face whitened. "These people are just so cruel. They haunted every step we took after we left Cadee and Benen. I understand they even set you two up."

"They did. Fortunately for them, we were aware of what was going on. The lady who first approached us has disappeared. The police in that country are on the look out for her but don't expect to find her."

Brandon pulled into his parking space. "I know we didn't have time to bring you here before the concert. You wanted to hear that. Let's get you in and get you settled. Tomorrow, Barnabas wants to meet with you two early in the morning. He knows you're the right ones this time, but he wants to talk with you. Our police chief wants to sit in."

"We have no problem with that. In fact, if he hadn't asked, I would have asked. Is it still Will?"

“It is. Do you know him?”

“I would say I do. We’re old friends. He just doesn’t tell people that.” Ted reached for his bags, drawing back his hand as the two younger men shook their heads and then pointed towards the door.

Chapter 34

Benen finally arose from his computer, stretching to release the muscles that had tensed. He had been afraid that he would be far behind in his work, but surprisingly he hadn't been. He would need to find out which one of his friends had stepped in. He knew one of them had. He had heard Cadee on the violin at different times over the morning and felt soothed by the hymns she had played. She was quiet now, and that concerned him, sending him looking for her. He found her in the living room, curled up on the couch, her Bible open on her knee, but her eyes raised to his.

"Benen? When you were captive, did you pray or could you pray?"

He sat down at the end of the couch, tucking the blanket around her feet. "What do you mean?"

"I mean, you're a praying man. Did you pray?"

"I guess I did. It's so automatic with me that I have no doubt I did. Why ask that?"

She shrugged. "I have no idea. I've been reading about how God protects us and just wondered if you had prayed. I know we were all praying for you. The church had a prayer chain going all day and night. But it's different when you're in the midst of the difficulty. We're told to pray, but sometimes our words are not audible or we can't."

"That's when the Holy Spirit steps in and prays for us. Brady said he prayed but he felt a presence with us. We should have frozen or been hypothermic but weren't. Now, you tell me, how did that happen?"

"God!" She turned her head as the door bell rang. "Of course, someone would interrupt us at this point."

Benen laughed. "We'll talk again. You have raised an interesting question." His hand on the open door, he froze, unable to speak, staring at the couple standing there, their eyes on his face, not quite sure of their reception.

"Ted. Mary. I didn't know you were back." He reached to hug them, and then pointed towards the living room. "Cadee's in there."

"Thank you, Benen." Ted was overcome with emotions for a moment. "We can't thank you enough for getting our girl out."

Benen shrugged, embarrassed for a moment, before he heard Cadee's feet on the floor as she headed his way.

"Benen? Which one of the guys is here and won't come in all the way?" She appeared in the hallway, stopping, her hands to her mouth in surprise. "Mom? Dad? Is that really you this time?"

Benen began to laugh. "It's really them. We can ask for ID but I don't think we'll need it."

Cadee shook a finger at him. "Not funny, buster." She turned back to her mother, hesitant about going near her.

"Cadee Rose, come here, dear. It really is your mother this time. I understand I had a stand-in that wasn't such a hot item."

Cadee began to laugh as she reached for her mother, hugging tightly before she turned to her father. "Yep, it's you. When did you get in?"

"In time enough to hear a girl play a violin."

"You were there, Dad? I didn't see you." Cadee backed up to Benen, finding his arms around her.

"That was the plan, dear. Barnabas didn't want us together last night. He wanted to talk to us first." Mary looked around the suite. "This is nice, Benen. I know it's not your regular one, but this is really nice."

"And just where are you?" Cadee's eyes narrowed as she headed into the kitchen.

"Right above this one, I think." Mary moved to help her daughter. "We'll talk, Cadee. We will talk when we get a chance. Both of us have been through too much."

"I know, Mom. That I know." She shared a look with Benen, not seeing the look her parents shared, or the relief that they felt shown on their faces. "What time does Barnabas expect to meet with us all?"

Mary's mouth dropped open before she snapped it closed. "Cadee, that's not nice."

She shrugged, a smile on her face. "Barnabas knows me. He knew I would ask that." She dug an elbow into Benen who had moved to stand right behind her. "Benen, stop your laughing. We have serious things to talk about."

"We do at that, my darling. We do, but as Breck says, you bring a sense of levity to the situation that is so needed."

She paused, then nodded. "You are all so sober. Berneen and I have to do that."

Barnabas looked up from his desk as Amy entered the office, shutting the door behind her.

"Amy?" He peered around her at the closed door.

She was laughing almost too hard to talk. "Cadee's here and in fine form. She just asked me if you were ready to meet with them and just what did you have to say this time?"

Barnabas had begun to grin as Amy started talking, the grin turning to laughter. "She's a character. Benen and she make a great pair."

"They do. Let's pray this adventure or misadventure or whatever you want to call it ends soon. They need to get on with their lives. And Ted and Mary? Just where do you see them in the Foundation work?"

"Got me there, didn't you? I've been praying about that. The director of the homeless shelter told me a couple of days ago he needs to move back to Alberta to be with family that are unwell. I feel Ted and Mary would do well there, but I need to pray more about that and then talk to him."

"Perfect. Just the ones we need." She turned to open the door. "But are you ready to face Cadee?"

<hr>

She smirked at him as he laughed and said to send them in.

Chapter 35

Barnabas watched with amusement as Cadee entered his office, seeking the chair she normally sat in. Her parents were more hesitant, Ted nodding at him before Cadee pointed to chairs for them. Benen was behind him, laughter on his face, his hands raised in a helpless manner as he caught Barnabas' grin.

"Good morning, Cadee." Barnabas moved to a chair beside her. "Thank you for last night. You added just the right touch to the concert for the families. We have been inundated with calls asking who was playing."

She shrugged. "I guess you can tell them. But that's not why I did it."

"We all know that, Cadee." Benen reached for her hand. "But I think we need to turn our attention now to what's going on with us."

Cadee shuddered. "I know we do. I wish it was all over with. Barnabas?"

"We're working on that. Will should be here shortly. He wants to update us. And no, he could send his detective but he wants to do the updating. This spans more than one country and continent and he has to be involved."

Cadee stared at him. "It does, doesn't it?"

"What does?"

"More than one country. More than one continent. What did I go and get involved in. Or rather, what did we?"

Ted spoke. "It does, Cadee. And we may need to go back to that country." He turned to Barnabas. "What do you have on the mission?"

"What you suspect, I think. It was taken over, all the others were sent home, except for you three. We're starting to get a sense of why, but not definite enough that we can go to anyone for an investigation."

"We were told about the couple. That's sad, but how do they relate to us? If they do." Ted watched his daughter as he spoke.

"Plastic surgery to make them look more like you. Cadee, I think you were picking up on something with them."

"I did. I felt evil around them and couldn't figure it out. Not from my parents." She looked up at Benen. "Benen?"

He nodded. "There was something." He looked around as Will entered. "Good morning, Will."

"Good morning, all." Will slid into a seat, his eyes on Ted and Mary. "The right ones, this time?"

Cadee began to laugh. "They are. God brought them back, protected them. They tell me they felt His hand many times over."

They fell silent at that point, before Ted began to pray. Cadee looked around as he finished, knowing that their adventure, as she termed it, would soon be over, she prayed and hoped. They couldn't go on much longer, she thought.

Will wasn't able to give much more details than they already knew. "That house, Benen? It is connected to that couple. His father owned it before it was abandoned. So they are local to the area. Their names are not for release at this time."

"That's fair." Benen finally rose, and reached for Cadee's hand. "If that's all, I need to be at work. Cadee has volunteered to help." He grinned down at her as she stared at him. "You promised to play those hymns again for me. And we have that discussion on prayer to continue."

She rose, her hand in his. "If you insist. Mom and Dad? I'm not sure about lunch but can we get together for supper?"

"We can do that, Cadee." Ted watched until the younger couple had walked away and the door had closed before he spoke. "Okay, Will. What are you not saying?"

Will stared at the closed door before he finally spoke. "I know you, Ted. Barnabas, we've talked. There are contracts out on Cadee and now Benen. Who put the one on Benen is still unknown, but with him being abducted like he was, they are serious. We need to put a better guard around them. At least until we can identify who is it."

Barnabas nodded. "The guys are pushing here, trying to find out any information they can for you. Branigan is just back from his conference and I know he'll be putting long hours of his own time."

Ted nodded, his eyes on Will. "Will?"

"We need to talk, Ted. Do you have any idea of who it was in the mission that set you up down there?"

Ted shook his head, his eyes on Mary. "We don't. We've done our best to find out, but down there, it's totally different. You would never find out by asking. That's a given."

Will sighed. "That is about what I thought you would say."

Chapter 36

Branigan walked towards Benen's office the next morning, a puzzled look on his face. He had been away at a conference and had just returned late the night before. He had spoken with Breck, who had brought him up to date on what was happening with Benen and Cadee. He had stared at Breck, shock on his face.

"Benen too? What is going on?"

"That is what we're not sure of, Branigan. We'll want you to go through Benen's place. The police did, but we'll feel better knowing one of our guys has done that." Breck had paused at that point. "You know that Ted and Mary are back. Cadee is still hesitant about them. I can understand why."

"To tell the truth, so would I be. How is Benen handling all this?"

Breck shrugged. "He's quiet, not saying much. But then again, that's him."

"It is. Do you know where I can find him?"

"Likely in his office. He's been working there some and in the suite a lot as well, just to be near Cadee. Now that Cadee! She has a wicked sense of humour."

Branigan just shook his head as he walked away, finding Blair waiting for him.

———

163

"You're heading to find Benen?" Blair's question raised Branigan's eyebrows.

"I am. Why?"

"Because I need to talk to him. I had his vehicle in the shop." Blair held out a hand. "I found this on his brakes."

"What?" Branigan looked at that. "What is it?"

"I'm not sure, but I don't think it was placed there for his health."

Branigan's face hardened as they walked towards Benen's office. "This is getting worse and worse, Blair. Breck talked to me this morning."

"Good. Then you're up to speed on what's going on."

Branigan paused at Benen's office door, a prayer rising from within him. He could feel danger approaching his friend.

Benen looked around and waved at his two friends, motioning towards his computer. They nodded, knowing he would be with them as soon as he was able. Branigan wandered the office, feeling something odd about it but not sure what.

The two men had finally found seats, hearing Benen's voice as he worked with a client. Their heads turned as the door opened and Cadee came in, a tray in her hands that she placed on Benen's desk, a quick kiss to his cheek, and then she was gone.

Branigan stared after her before turning to Blair, finding his face alight with laughter.

"Cadee?"

"She's like that, Branigan. She's quiet when she needs to be. I understand this has become a habit, that if Benen is here working, she'll bring a tray mid-morning for him." Blair rose as he heard Benen moving about in his office. "How did she know?"

"How did she know what?" Branigan stared in turn at the tray. "She brought enough for all of us?"

"She did." Benen reached to shake Branigan's hand. "Don't ask how she knows. She does. She can put a finger on the pulse in this building and find the one who needs her help."

"She's been here, what about two weeks?" Blair took the mug offered him and then studied the plate of goodies Cadee had left.

"About that. She knew you two were here. Ask her sometime how she knows. She can't explain it."

Blair nodded before he dropped the object he had been holding on Benen's desk. "Know what this is, Benen?"

Benen stared at Blair for a moment and then down, finally reaching to pick up the object. He sighed. "I do. Ted showed me one when I was down there. Where'd you find it?"

"On your brakes. It was meant to take them out." Blair was growing angry, not at Benen, but at the culprits responsible for this.

"My brakes?" Benen sat back, his eyes thoughtful. "Which one was he after?"

"What do you mean?" Branigan leaned forward, his mug down on the desk.

"Cadee drives it sometimes. In fact, she asked this morning if you were done with it, Blair."

Blair paled. "I was until something nudged me to check the brakes. It wasn't due for that, just the oil change." He looked around as the door opened and Cadee reappeared.

"Benen, is your vehicle ready? Mom and I want to head into town." She stopped as she saw the two men sitting there and then her eyes were drawn to the object Benen still held. "Benen? Where did you get that? I thought I left all those explosive devices behind me."

"Obviously not. It was on the brakes of my car."

She paled and then nodded. "Of course it would be. They are obviously not done with us, are they?" She tamped down the anger she felt. "Guys, talk to Dad. He might have an idea of who, but don't count on it."

Benen watched her closely, seeing the fear she was trying hard to hide. "Cadee, we can get you two into town. In fact, I'll borrow a vehicle and take you."

She just shook her head and walked away, leaving the three men staring after her.

"Did she just do that?" Blair's head turned back to Benen.

He sighed. "She did. Now, she won't go, and I know Ted and Mary need things." He rose, his eyes on his computer. "I can leave for a while, but I have a conference call in two hours. That won't give much time."

Branigan and Blair shared a look before Branigan spoke. "I booked today off, Benen, knowing I'd get in late. Let me take them."

Benen finally nodded. "Let me go get her and you can talk to her." He turned, finding Cadee right behind him, fear on her face. "Cadee?"

She held out her hand, a small box in it. "I found this in our kitchen, Benen. Who put it there?"

The three men crowded around her, Benen's arm holding her close to him, as they peered into the box.

"What is that?" Blair's voice was low and unsure.

"It's a warning. That's what it is. It's similar to what you pulled off Benen's car, only it goes on a door to a house. This was sitting on the counter. Someone has been in our place, Benen. How?"

Chapter 37

His face grim, Barnabas stood in the conference room, watching his men as they milled around before finding places at the table. The news that someone had been in Benen's apartment has disturbing, but finding someone had made their way into the secure suite was even more disturbing. His security captain was running videos trying to find the exact time the explosive object was left, but he had not heard back from him. He suspected that they wouldn't, that a blip would be found in the security feed for the length of time it took the person to get in and out. There was also the security log from the door. Branigan had taken a look at it and then shook his head. Again, someone seemed to have hacked into their system, and they had one of the best available.

He finally sat, staring down at the folder in front of him, before he looked up, seeing Buckley. Buckley nodded, his head bowing as he led them in prayer. They all knew that only God would provide the answers they sought and the protection that was needed.

"Branigan, where do we stand?" Barnabas' question came quickly after their heads were raised.

Branigan shook his head. "About where you expected. Someone hacked into our systems. I have a friend who is working on tracing it. I'm not sure if he'll be able to."

“Okay. Benen?” Barnabas watched as Benen's attention returned to the room. "Did you talk to Ted?”

“I did, but he can't help. He hasn't seen those before. He was puzzled that Cadee had. I asked her. She said the boys in her Bible class showed one to her, warned her to watch for them. They didn't tell her why, but she took it as a warning. She's shaken, Barnabas. And it takes a lot to shake her.”

Bradon looked across the table at Benen. "She's asked about getting a dog. Did you know that?”

Benen nodded. "I do. We had talked about that but decided not to at this point. I'm not all that convinced that she wants one.” He looked around at his friends, knowing they would do their best to solve this and protect his lady.

Finally rising, no further ahead with information or planning, Benen walked away, heading for Cadee, not finding her. That didn't surprise him. She was likely with Mary or Ted he thought.

He stood for a moment in the kitchen, a frown on his face, wondering just how safe Cadee was, wherever she happened to be at the moment. He turned as he heard the door open and close, and then Cadee's voice muttering to herself.

Cadee stopped, a smile lighting her face as she saw Benen.

“Benen? Are you working? You can't be done for the day?”

“No, I'm not. I just needed to make sure you were okay.” He paused and then shook his head. “I have to head into town now for the camera club meeting. Want to come with me?"

She shrugged. "No, not really. I think I'll just relax."

He studied her for a moment, seeing the fatigue and whiteness on her face. "You've been doing too much." He walked towards her, reaching to hug her. "That's okay. I don't need to go."

"No, you need to. The club needs you to."

Late that afternoon, Benen quietly closed the door, toeing off his shoes to leave on the boot tray and hanging up his jacket in the closet. Low lights shone in the apartment and he moved slowly through it, looking for Cadee. He frowned when he didn't find her. Searching again, he saw nothing that showed him where she was.

A soft sound had him spinning, heading for the walk-in closet in the bedroom. Shoving open the door, he reached for the light switch, flooding the area. He frowned, not seeing anything, before he searched again.

Phone in his hand, he headed for the door, knowing it had been locked, before he spun, heading for the French doors in the living room that led to the outside. Unlocked! He frowned once more as he stepped through.

"Ted?" He spoke into the phone as Ted answered. "Is Cadee with you?"

"She was but headed home about ten minutes ago. Why?"

"She's not here."

"What? I walked her down and went in with her to check." Ted's voice faded for a moment. "I'm on my way down."

Benen clicked off his phone, watching the early night sky for answers before he looked down, a sound coming from him as he ran across the patio, intent on finding Cadee. Following footprints, he slid to a halt, his heart in his mouth at the dark object in front of him. Dropping to his knees, he carefully rolled the person over, fearful that it was Cadee. It was Mike, the night security guard.

Benen was on his feet, his phone out to call Barnabas as he heard his name called. Swinging around, he found Bradon there, Kade beside him, his hackles raised as he stared off into the night.

"Benen?"

"It's Mike. I can't find Cadee. Ted walked her down to the apartment about fifteen minutes ago. She's not there." Benen spun suddenly, a cry sounding in his ears and was running for the lakeshore, Kade in front of him, ears back, a low growl coming from him.

Bradon stood for a moment in shock, watching his dog run from him without being sent, and then he was racing after them, not seeing some of the other men who had heard the commotion and came from their apartments.

Brandon, Blair and Burney were after Benen and Bradon as quickly as their feet could take them. Brady was on his knees beside Mike, helping him to sit up, turning as Breck crouched down beside him.

"He's okay?"

Mike nodded. "I am. I was blindsided. I saw Cadee being hauled away and came to help her. I didn't see the other man." He shifted, frantic to find her. "Where is she?"

"She's not here. Benen and Bradon are after her." Brady helped him to his feet. "Let's get you in and get you assessed."

Mike shifted away from him. "Go after them. They can't have gotten far. They were heading for the lake."

Brady stared at him before Mike shoved him. "Go. If she's hurt, she'll need you. I'll find Doc if I have to."

Brady shook his head and then was running as well, hearing shouts from in front of him, sliding to a stop as he saw Benen and Bradon standing still, hands in the air and then his focus went past them to where Cadee stood, a man's arm around her keeping her still, a knife held to her neck.

Chapter 38

Barnabas watched from behind the pile of rocks, knowing others of his men were around, and that a call had gone in to the police department for assistance. It was a question whether they would make it in time. He watched as Kade circled, his eyes on Cadee, whom Barnabas knew he adored, just waiting for an opportunity to take down the man holding her. Barnabas turned as he felt a hand on his shoulder. Buckley stood there.

"Can we move in?"

Barnabas shook his head. "Not yet. He's keeping that knife on her." He tried to see through the darkening sky. "If we don't though, he'll be gone in the darkness."

Buckley nodded. "I know. Blair, Brandon and Brody are heading around them with the huge spotlights we have. That should help."

They ducked as the lights suddenly lit up the night, causing the man who was holding Cadee to jump. Benen watched carefully, seeing her flinch, and made a move towards her, stopping as something in the tree line caught his eyes, before he shook his head. He wasn't sure he had even seen anything there. He heard Bradon give a soft sound and his attention was back on Cadee.

No words were uttered by the man holding her as his gaze was locked with Benen's once more. Benen frowned, thinking he knew the man but then shook his head. He didn't, did he? He watched closely, see the fear Cadee was trying her best to hide. Then, the man began backing towards the water, wading into the icy cold lake, dragging Cadee with her. She began to struggle, the shock of the water moving her to try to escape. She shoved at the man's hand, pushing it away before she kicked at his shin, loosening his grip. She shoved away from him and dove into the water, her breath gone at the cold, and tried her best to swim. She didn't hear Benen's shout or Bradon's yell at Kade.

As soon as Cadee had started her move, Kade had crept closer, his eyes intent on the man. And then he sprang, his powerful jaws clamping on the arm still holding the knife, taking the man down on the sand.

Benen gave a shout, his feet pounding across the sand, trying to see where Cadee was. He plunged into the water, diving down, frantic to find her. Surfacing, he heard the calls from his friends and then he saw Brody heading for shore, Cadee's limp motionless form in his arms. He plunged through the water, not caring that he was soaked, stumbling as he hit the sand, catching his balance and then running towards his bride. He didn't feel the blanket draped around him as he dropped to his knees, his hands reaching for her, fighting the hands that held him back.

Pulled to his feet and back from where she lay, he struggled to get back to her, but his arms were held in a firm grip. Buckley stood on one side of him, Brennen on the other, their eyes full of concern, their faces grim. Their grips tightened on him.

———

Brady was on his knees beside Cadee, working frantically to revive her, doing CPR, Doc on his knees with him. They could hear the sounds of the sirens and then the calls of the responding officers and emergency personnel.

Brady looked up as the paramedics dropped beside him.

"She was in the lake. Not for long, maybe five minutes at the most." He continued his work before stepping aside and letting the paramedics take over, his body turning so he could search for Brody and then Benen. Brody shook him off, nodding towards Benen.

"Look after him, Brady."

"You're okay?"

Brody shrugged, pulling the blanket around him tighter. "I'm okay. I'll get someone to take me in but I'm fine. Benen needs you."

Benen stood, desperate to be with Cadee, watching as the men and women worked around them, hearing Barnabas talking to someone, asking that they find Ted and Mary and get them to the hospital. He watched as Cadee was lifted to a stretcher, a blanket wrapped tight around her before he broke free and moved with the stretcher, his hand on her arm. He refused to back away when she was loaded into the rig, hopping up and sitting in a corner, his eyes on her, not taking in the continued activity. He was vaguely aware that Brady was with them.

Benen stood once more, blanket still around him, his arms folded, leaning against the wall in the Emergency Department, his eyes on the room where they had taken Cadee, his mind echoing with the words he had heard. They didn't know if she'd awaken, or how she would be. The lake water had been frigid and that concerned them all.

Doc watched for a moment before he nodded to Barnabas and both men walked towards Benen. Benen's eyes never moved from the room door.

"Benen?" Doc's voice finally brought his eyes around. "Here. You need to get into dry clothes."

Shaking his head, Benen refused to move. "I can't. I need to see her."

"They won't let you in. Not yet. They're working on her." Doc's hand was firm on his shoulder, turning him and then gently shoving him into a room. "Change and then I'll be back to assess you. The ER physician told me to."

Benen stared at the closing door before he stared down at the bag holding his dry clothes. Lord, save her, please. I can't go on if she doesn't make it. He knew full well what Doc and Brady hadn't said. He remembered losing a friend to hypothermia when he was a teenager. That was his fear. That he would lose his lady love.

Chapter 39

His hand holding open the door, Barnabas watched as Benen paced the exam room. He knew Doc had been back in, warning Benen not to leave, that someone would be around to examine him, shaking off his protests.

"It will be done, Benen, and soon. You were in the lake. As was Brody. He's been assessed and cleared. I can tell you this much. If you refuse, they will not let you in to see Cadee. They need to ensure you are not harmed." Doc had stared him down, compassion on his face.

Benen swung as he heard the door open, his eyes hopeful, then his face whitening as he saw the grim and sober looks on Barnabas and Buckley's faces. His head began to shake as he backed away, until the bed behind him stopped his movements.

Barnabas halted his steps, knowing that they had frightened Benen without intending to.

"No, they're working on her still, Benen. I'm sorry. I didn't mean to frighten you." Barnabas shared a look with Buckley.

"Can I see her?" Benen felt like he was begging, but he just wanted to be with her.

"In about ten minutes or so." Buckley's hand rested on his friend. "First, we need to pray for you both."

Benen stared at him, his thoughts muddled, a puzzled look on his face, before he nodded, his head bowing.

His head raised as the door opened and a physician entered, Doc walking beside him.

"Benen?" Doc spoke first. "This is George Forrest. He's been treating Cadee."

"Doctor?" He studied the man in front of him, a man near Doc's age he thought. "Cadee?"

"She's starting to warm up, Benen. It will be a while. We'll take you in to her but be prepared for all sorts of lines and machines. It's standard." He shared a look with Doc. "But there is one thing you need to be aware of."

Benen waited, not sure what was going on. "Doctor? What aren't you telling me?" He shifted his focus to the door, seeing the light green of the walls, the various equipment in his peripheral vision.

"Her throat was sliced, likely when she made her move to escape." Barnabas's hand steadied Benen as the physician continued. "It wasn't deep but deep enough to be of concern."

Benen moved away from Barnabas, shaking off his hand, intent on finding Cadee, not hearing the voices calling him to wait. He almost ran from the room, pulling the door open in an almost violent manner, heading for the room where Cadee was, pausing for a moment before he opened the door, his eyes focused on her, his feet moving forward without a conscious thought on his part.

He didn't focus on the equipment surrounding her, the hum and deep of the equipment itself, the moving of the nursing staff as they worked. His focus was strictly on her, his hand reaching to touch her face, mindful of the oxygen line that lay across her cheeks. He blinked rapidly, willing the tears not to fall. He ignored the sound of the rubber soled shoes moving around him, the swish of the door as it opened and closed, and the footsteps that moved to stand beside him. He didn't raise his eyes to study the light creams walls. His vision remained locked on Cadee.

"Benen?" Doc's quiet voice had him turning his head to the older man.

"Doc?"

"You heard George. She's a survivor. But what she went through a couple of weeks ago has affected her recovery today. She was still not over the poisoning."

Benen just stared at him, before his attention went back to Cadee. "Did they catch the guy?"

"The one who had her? They did. Kade kept him down until the police could move in. The man's not talking though."

"He knew Cadee. I could see it in his face." He looked up, frowning at the heart monitor. "I just don't understand why she was outside. Did Mike say anything?"

"No. He didn't see anything, but his impression was that there was more than one man. He vaguely recalls seeing Cadee being dragged towards the lake."

Barnabas' voice sounded from behind him. "That's what we can't understand. Why the lake?"

"A boat?"

"That's what Will said they were looking into. But there's no proof a boat was out there." Barnabas was frustrated. "The man's not from here."

"I didn't think he would be. He seemed familiar to him. I think I might have seen him hanging around the mission." Benen sighed even as his hand rested on Cadee's cheek, feeling the chill in her skin. "That means he won't speak much English."

"Will thought of that. He's bringing in an interpreter but the only one available on short notice is Brenden."

"And that's a conflict of interest right here, isn't it?" Benen turned to face his friends, his eyes rising to the door where Ted and Mary stood, hesitant about entering. He walked towards them and into Mary's hug, Ted's arm around the two before they headed back to the bedside.

Chapter 40

Cadee stared at Benen two days later as he stood in front of her, a mug of tea extended. She had insisted on moving home, telling the physicians that was what she wanted. She hated the hospital, it reminded her too much of the episode just a couple of weeks ago. Her eyes moved away from Benen, studying the living room of yet another suite they had been moved to, this time on the second floor of the building. She decided the pale amber of the walls was suitable but not her and not Benen. Nor was the leather furniture. She disliked the TV on the wall. She was nitpicking, she knew but just couldn't help herself.

Benen watched her closely before he sighed and walked away, knowing she wanted to fight and just not wanting to do that. He stood where he could watch her, seeing her shove herself back onto the couch before he approached, dropping a blanket over her despite her protests.

"You need this, Cadee. Now, the doctor said light food. Anna brought in some as did your mother. What would you like?"

She glared at him, her arms crossed, not happy with her situation.

"Give it a rest, Cadee. These are orders. What would you like? If you don't tell me, I'll find something and then stand over you until you finish it." Benen was losing patience with the situation, and didn't need Cadee's stubbornness.

She refused to answer him, her eyes daring him to follow through on his threat. He shook his head, knowing they needed to talk, but right now, she wouldn't. Lord, please? Protect her. Show me, show us, how we do just that. I'm at a loss to know just how. He meditated on that as he prepared a tray with soup, jello and the tea she favoured, setting it on a table beside her before he sat once more at the end of the couch, his mug of coffee on the table, tucking her feet under the blanket, one hand resting on her ankle, the other elbow on the back of the couch as his hand rested on his cheek, his eyes on her.

She finally reached for the mug of soup, knowing she did have to eat, but with little appetite.

"Who all was hurt that night?" Her question when it came was not unexpected.

"Mike has knocked out but is fine. Brody went into the lake as did I. He's the one who found you. And then there's Kade."

"Kade? What do you meant?" She sipped at her soup, a perplexed look on her face.

"He left Bradon behind, running after you. He broke his trust with Bradon to do that. He crept around and then attacked the man without being commanded to because you were in trouble. He has never done that before, and now Bradon is not sure how much he can trust him."

Cadee looked shocked. "He did what? Why?"

"Because it was you. Because to him, you're family and he has to look after his family." Benen's hand tightened on her foot. "And in doing that, he broke his training. He should have waited to be sent out and didn't."

Cadee was shocked. "I didn't know he'd do that. I mean, I never went overboard with anything to do with him. I only would pet him or play with him if Bradon said it was okay."

"We know, my darling. We know. Now, that man?"

She shuddered. "That man." She refused to look at him.

"Cadee, my darling. I know you know him. He's refusing to speak. Who is he?"

She sighed, finally setting her mug aside and wrapping her arms around herself. "I know his first name. It's Juan. But I don't know anything else about him. I don't even know if Dad or Mom saw him hanging around the mission. He watched me all the time. I think that's part of what Dad was warned about. But I don't know why he was there." She lifted eyes that were frightened and distressed.

Benen nodded. "That is what Will thought. That he was someone from down there. But why did he do what he did." He watched as she shuddered again. "What did he say?"

She shook, her hands clenching at the blanket. "I can't."

Benen's head came around as he heard the doorbell and he rose with a muttered sound. "This is not over, Cadee. Not by a long shot."

He stood at the open door, eyeing Will and Barnabas and then Ted. "Come on in. I'll need your help."

"For what?" Will dropped his coat on the table in the entryway.

"Cadee's given me a name. She just won't tell me what he said. And she needs to."

"Cadee?" Will's voice brought her head around and she blanched, knowing she would need to confess what was said. "What's this I hear?"

"What did you hear?" She was playing for time and refused to meet her father's eyes.

"Cadee Rose. Enough. If you can tell us what was said, it will help. It may mean the difference between life and death for you, for Benen, for any of us. They showed that the other night when they attacked Mike. They could have very easily killed him."

She finally nodded, her eyes on Benen, who had at back down at her feet. "He told me I had to go with him. That I belonged to someone else. That if I didn't, he would kill Benen."

Her words caused the men to draw in their breath sharply, their eyes first on her and then on one another.

"Ted? Did you know that?" Will's voice was harsh.

"No, I didn't. I wish I had. I would have taken steps long before I did. I had heard rumours that the drug lord had his eye on someone but never heard a name."

Chapter 41

Cadee refused to look at the men, before Benen was on his feet, pulling her up and then sitting back with her wrapped in his arms. He felt her shudders.

"Cadee? He wasn't alone."

She shook her heard. "No, he wasn't. He grabbed me when I stepped out on the patio for a breath of air. I shouldn't have. I knew that, but I had seen Mike just walking by and thought I was safe." Her shudders deepened. "He had me before I could move. I knew there was another man. I could hear them talking but I couldn't understand what they were saying. I didn't know the language."

"Why didn't you tell me that before?" Will's voice though firm was still gentle.

She shrugged. "I couldn't. I didn't know who would hear me."

The men finally left, Ted lingering a moment to watch Cadee, who refused to look at him, her focus on her hands. Benen walked him to the door.

"What do we do now, Ted?" Benen was worried, knowing that one of the men was still out there.

"Pray and pray hard. You need to work. You can't be with her all the time. We'll pick up where we can. Barnabas is talking to his security team to see what they can do." He sighed. "But she will fight us all on that."

"Not if I can help it. Just pray this is over. Christmas is in ten days. I would like to enjoy our first Christmas without this over our heads." He turned to look back towards Cadee. "Barnabas has said we can move home tomorrow. That may help."

Cadee was no where to be found when Benen returned and he went looking for her, hearing the shower running and knowing she needed that time. He headed for the kitchen, tidying it for the night, before he reached for his laptop. He had to work. There were some calls that needed to be returned, only he had no heart for that tonight. Instead, he reached for his Bible, searching for words of comfort, of peace, of strength, knowing he would need them if he wanted to protect his lady. His head bowed in prayer, he didn't hear Cadee until her hand caught his as she sat beside him, her own head bowing.

The next afternoon, Cadee wandered Benen's apartment, not sure what she should be doing. Benen, she knew, was hard at work in his office and she was trying to be quiet for him. She turned as she heard a tap at the door and cautiously approached it, peeking out to see Berneen and Mary standing there. She pulled opened the door, her mouth dropping open as she saw the tree Berneen was holding.

"We've come to bring cheer." Mary reached to hug her daughter. "Now, tell us where you want it. You two girls can decorate." She held up the bag she was holding. "I'm baking, something I've wanted to do for five years."

Benen's head lifted for a moment later that morning as he heard the ladies' laughter and smiled. This would do Cadee good. He would need to talk to her later. Barnabas had called as had Will. Their news had not been good.

Cadee leaned back on Benen late that afternoon as his arms came around her.

"You're done for the day?" She had a wistful note to her voice.

"I am. The house looks nice." He looked around at the decorations. "You had fun."

"I did. Berneen is such a character. And her brother was by, as well."

"Darby? I thought he had school all day."

"He was off. Something about teachers striking."

"That's right. They are." He turned her towards the couch, gently shoving her down before his arm was around her as he sat beside her. "Will and Barnabas both called."

"They did?" She studied his face. "It's not good news."

"No, it's not. Somehow the man who captured you killed himself last night. They're investigating but they can't figure it out. No one was in to see him. The guards were by every ten to fifteen minutes."

"Well, that's that then. I would gather that he didn't speak."

"No, he didn't. But something has puzzled me. Why back into the lake and take you with him? Was that part of his original plan?" His head tilted at he watched her.

She shook for a moment before she rubbed at her face. "I think he was supposed to go down the beach, or up the beach. Towards my right. Then he saw you two. I heard him muttering in whatever language that was and he started to pull me backwards." She twisted to look at him. "Did Dad know anything?"

Benen hesitated to speak, his mouth opening before he closed it, trying to gather his thoughts.

"Benen? What did he say?"

Benen finally looked down at her, trying to figure out how to protect her. "He said he had heard rumours of a drug lord or someone like that and a young lady, he could never determine exactly who or why. And that bothers him."

"I had heard the same rumours. Those kind of rumours are rampant down there, as you can well imagine." She looked down before she raised her eyes again. "You looked away from me that night and to your left. Why?"

He shook his head. "There was something or someone there. I couldn't get enough of a look to know for sure. Just an impression."

"And those impressions are usually right." She sighed, her head coming down on his shoulder. "When will this end, Benen? When will it end?"

———

Chapter 42

Standing in the church entryway on the following Sunday, Cadee watched for Benen to enter, her thoughts really not on being there. She had felt someone following her whenever she had left the building for the last few days, and it didn't help that Benen made sure someone was with her, one of his friends or one of the security people. She shook her head. He seemed to be taking things too far, she thought. She felt eyes on her and looked around, not seeing anyone who didn't seem to belong.

Benen stood at the entrance, deep in conversation with Jace, his eyes on Cadee. Something was up with her, he thought, before he finally excused himself, and walked over to her. An arm around her, he led her away from the crowds.

"Cadee? What's going on?" His voice was full of concern as was his face.

She shrugged, feeling herself growing more and more tense. "Someone is here, Benen, and I don't know who or why." She looked up at him and he drew in a sharp breath at the fear in her eyes. "It's coming to a head, as Dad says. I don't want anyone else hurt, but I don't seem to be able to prevent that."

"None of us seem to be able to do that." He bit at his lip as he looked around. "Do you want to stay or leave?"

"We can't leave! What would Buckley think?" She was horrified at his question.

"He would understand completely. He's like that." Benen watched her face closely before he sighed to himself, wrapped an arm around her and led her to the pew at the back he usually sat in. Brady stood and let them sit before he sat back down, leaning forward to watch Cadee before he looked at Benen, who simply shook his head.

Cadee tried hard to listen to Buckley, but her mind kept wandering. She tucked her hand into Benen's and felt his grip tighten on her. Buckley's word finally reached to her and she sat up and listened. Not a normal Christmas message, she thought.

Buckley's voice resonated through the sanctuary, causing the congregation to exchange puzzled glances. What he was saying? They had never thought of it before. They had never thought how God had protected Mary, protected Joseph. To have traveled in those times, he said, would have been a risk. It was not like today, where they could travel in a vehicle. Cadee thought about that, realizing that God did provide protection. She was sure He had with her.

She stood close to Benen as she waited for him to make the move to leave, not sure why he wasn't.

"Benen? It's over. Are we leaving?"

Benen shook his head. "Not yet. Branigan found something on our vehicle and wants us to wait." He turned slightly to watch her, seeing the sunlight reflecting through the stained glass windows on her face.

She stared at him, finally snapping her mouth closed. "When did he tell you that?"

"Just as the last song was finishing. You didn't see him?" He frowned as he watched her, not sure what was going on with her.

She shook her head. "No, I didn't. I guess I was concentrating too hard on something else." She flopped back down on the pew. "How long will it take?"

Bene shook his head. "They're trying to keep us both safe, Cadee". He looked around from where he stood as he heard his name called.

Branigan approached him, slowly, a grim look on his face, Blair and Bradon keeping step with him.

"Branigan?" Benen's voice died away as he looked down at the hand Branigan extended. "What?"

"This box, Benen? Cadee? It was sitting on the hood of your car, Benen. A warning. We opened it. In it are pictures of the two of you, alone, together, with whoever they could find to take pictures of. The last one is a nasty one."

Benen didn't take his eyes from Branigan, but he felt Cadee leaning against him.

"Why is it nasty?" Her voice was calm, but Benen could feel the tremor in her body.

Branigan exchanged a look with Blair and Bradon, before he tilted the box so Benen and Cadee could see it.

"That's grave!" Cadee's voice was shocked.

"It is. It has Benen's name on it. They're after him now, Cadee, and we need to find out why."

Cadee's gasp echoed the sound from Benen. "Who?"

"That's what we want to know. Now, we're taking you two home. Your car has been impounded for now. I spoke with Will. He will have officers here shortly to escort us." Branigan walked away, leaving the four to stare after him.

Chapter 43

Cadee found herself tucked between the men, her hand tight in Benen's, as they walked out to Bradon's truck. She frowned as she saw the three police cruisers waiting.

"Isn't this overkill?"

"Bad choice of words, Cadee." Bradon shook his head at her. "That's what will happen if we don't take precautions, and even then, there's no guarantee that will even keep you safe. They've proven they can get to you."

She slid into the car, Benen on one side of her, Bradon on the other, Branigan and Blair in the front seat. Barnabas ducked his head to look in before he nodded at Branigan and backed away.

Barnabas watched the cars drive away, wondering if they would make it home safe, and if they did, how did they proceed. Will stood at his side.

"What now, Will? How do we do this? This is nothing like Brady and Berneen."

"It's never the same, no matter how many times we do this. For now, I'll have officers in the building, outside their door, in his office. They will go nowhere they are not escorted."

Barnabas nodded, knowing just how bad it could get. He turned to walk away, turning back as Will spoke.

"She's going to go after them, you know."

Barnabas stared at him. "What did you just say?"

"Cadee. She's not going to sit back and let them come after her or Benen. She'll go on the offensive and I would say by tomorrow. Whether or not she tells Benen and he agrees with her, that's another question." Will paused, his thoughts muddled for a moment, his eyes narrowing as he pondered just what to do. "She'll slip away from anyone I have with her."

"We'll watch, but I think you're right. I've called a meeting with all of the guys for this afternoon. Hopefully we can come up with a plan."

"Make sure Benen is included."

"That's a given. Any suggestions?" Barnabas pulled on his gloves as they walked towards their vehicles, his shoulders hunching slightly against the cold wind blowing in off the lake.

"You're aware of what needs to be done. I know that. We've talked. Just keep an eye on her, and that is going to be difficult with your guys working and volunteering."

"Their volunteer work is done until the new year, and some have time off this week. Their places of employment are closed." Barnabas hit the key fob to unlock his doors. "I am just afraid, Will. Afraid that they will use one of them against the other or go after her parents."

———

"And that they will do." Will paused. "I can send someone out today to sit in on your meeting, if you like."

Barnabas nodded as he opened his door. "That would be appreciated. We're meeting in my office at about two." He smiled. "And I can almost guarantee Cadee will want to be there."

"You know, that's not a bad thought. Engage her. Get her involved. Don't hide from her what your plans are." Will waved as he walked away.

Barnabas stared down at the sandwich Cadee had handed him, a shuttered look on her face. He prayed for words, knowing he needed to reach her but not sure how.

"Barnabas? You're meeting with everyone?" Cadee's words roused hims attention from his prayer.

"I am, Cadee. If you would like to be there, you can." He watched her closely, her eyes on him before she nodded.

"I would like that. I've been thinking about this. I may have an idea who it is, and if it's him, God help us, is all I can say." She blinked rapidly before Benen gave a sound and wrapped an arm around her. She just shook her head at the question on his face. "I need to use your computer for a moment after we finish."

"I'll help you. Barnabas?" Benen looked over at him.

"We all will, Cadee. You are not alone in this. Neither is Benen. God has you in the hollow of His hand. The other guys are mad and want whoever this is. Will is sending someone this afternoon for our meeting. At the moment, he has officers stationed with you two at all times." Barnabas regretted his words as he saw Cadee's face pale even more than it was. "I'm sorry, Cadee. We have to do this. We have to figure out how to end this."

"He's right, my darling." Benen's arm tightened around her, even as his chin rested on her head before he bent and dropped a kiss there. "We can't go on like this."

"I know. I'm just so afraid. Where are we meeting?"

"I thought my office." Barnabas watched as Cadee shook her head. "Not there? Why? What are your thoughts?"

"Have you searched your office, Barnabas? Have any of you? Who's to say they haven't hidden things in there, just waiting for a time like this. Those guys from there are brutal. They have no respect for law and order." Cadee shoved back from the table and walked away, her feet taking her to the master bedroom where she sank to the side of the bed and bowed her head, struggling to control her emotions.

Benen had risen to his feet as she left, before he sat back down, his hands scrubbing down his face, fear in his eyes, before he looked over at Barnabas, seeing in his face a reflection of his own emotions.

"Barnabas, what are you thinking?"

"I'm thinking that she's likely correct in her assessment. And how do we plan for that, then?" Barnabas pulled his phone out and scanned the text message he received, his face growing grimmer.

———

"Will's had officers go over my office. Cadee was right. How did she know?"

"I have no idea. There will be people who say she's planned this herself." Benen turned his head to look towards the hallway. "I know she hasn't. No one knows the sleep she has lost, up pacing at night, tossing and turning, not sleeping except in fits and starts."

Barnabas snorted at his words. "I am sure they will. We know differently." He stopped, overcome with his emotions for a moment at the life his friends were forced to live. "I didn't realize it was that bad."

"She hasn't wanted to tell anyone, not even her parents. It has been draining." Benen rose, reaching for the coffee pot. "Where do we meet then?"

"Where they would least expect us. No one will be in today. We'll meet in the open. In the lobby. We'll be comfortable there. In the meantime, I will have Will send people to start searching our suites and offices. Our security guys can do that as well." He dropped his head into his hands for a moment. "I pray this ends with you two and the rest of us don't face something."

Chapter 44

Pulling her sweater tighter around her, Cadee slumped back into a corner of one of the couches in the lobby, her eyes on the fireplace. She watched the dancing flames, knowing it was a gas one, but still enjoying that vision. She didn't hear the men milling around her, or their quiet grim conversation. She jumped as she felt something touch her hand and looked down to find Kade standing there, his tongue out, his tail wagging. She stared at him before looking up, looking for Bradon. She was afraid to touch Kade, not wanting to interfere in his duty.

Bradon sat on the table in front of her, a grin on his face. "It's okay, Cadee. You can pet him. I've dealt with him taking off like that."

She shook her head and tucked her legs up, her eyes back on Kade. "No, I can't do that. Please?"

He shrugged and then called Kade back, who lay, his chin on his paws, his eyes on her. Bradon looked up as Benen sat beside Cadee.

"Benen?" He frowned at the look in Benen's eyes.

Benen shook his head. "They've been in all our suites, our offices. How?" He looked around, a frown on his face. "They have to have gotten to someone but who?"

"That's what we think. We're looking into that." Branigan spoke from where he had seated himself near them. "I don't think we'll be safe, any of us, until these people are caught."

"It's not just men, Branigan. Try women. Children. They will use whoever they can to get to us." Cadee shifted closer to Benen, her eyes rising as she heard footsteps heading their way. "Will's here. I thought you said he wouldn't be."

"He changed his mind when he was told what was found." Benen reached to hug her with one arm. "He's that worried, Cadee."

"Is he? What has he found out that he hasn't told us?" Cadee watched closely, seeing the worry on his face. "Will?"

Will just shook his head. He had news that he didn't want to share with her, but knew he needed to. "Cadee? Once we get started, let me speak. Then I have some questions for you."

She nodded, her eyes raising to Buckley as he stood, ready to pray for them all.

Will hesitated before he spoke, his thoughts on Cadee, his eyes on the folder he held before he handed it to her.

"Cadee, in this folder are photos I want you to look at." Will shook his head. "First, I have something to say and I need you to listen. Your response is important." He raised his eyes to Benen, finding him watching his bride closely.

"Will? You're scaring me." Cadee's voice was barely a whisper.

"That is the intent of what I am about to tell you and then show you. We have identified men and, yes, women who are involved in this plot against you. It is not what you have thought it was. There were rumours put out there that were meant to scare you and make you run. They had planned to take you and disappear when you did just that. But you didn't. You did the smart thing. You stayed with Benen or one of his friends, not letting them have a chance to get to you, other than that one time. They have been watching you closely. We have found evidence of that, not shared with anyone other than Barnabas. He has had security watching you both closely." Will paused, gathering his thoughts. "Your parents have been safe. They have not been targets. Now as to the reason, this is what we think. This is based on the investigations we have been pursuing. Our detective even made a trip down to the mission. He found some interesting data. That we can't share totally with you, but we'll share what we can."

He paused once more to sip at the mug of tea he had been handed, sorting through thoughts before he continued.

"Cadee, there was no drug lord down there looking for you. There wasn't anyone in that country looking for you. We have traced those rumours, with great difficulty, back here to Ontario. To the mission you worked under."

Cadee's mouth opened as she went to speak, and then snapped closed, anger on her face. "That mission again. When did the rumours start?"

"Just before the mission was taken over. We're working through that. Trust me. We want these people even more than you do. You're not the only one that has been targeted. I can't go into any details on that as it is an active investigation." He shook his head. "But, you. What they wanted? That's what we working through. You need to take all the precautions you can. Benen does as well. They will use him to get to you. Do you remember anything at all?"

Cadee shook her head, searching her thoughts. "There was one man who came down, said he was with the mission. That was in the summer. Dad and I questioned him closely. He couldn't or wouldn't say why he was there. We didn't know him, so we were really cautious in our dealings with him. He sent out strange vibes, if you want to call it that. I felt evil in him. Dad did too. He mentioned it in passing one day." She said a name, her eyes on Will as she did, seeing his nod. "You've been looking at him, haven't you? Is he in the area?"

"He is, Cadee. We have been asked by other forces to watch for him. He's not a very nice person. In fact, he is a very dangerous person. What we don't know is how he managed to take over the mission." Will looked around. "All I can say is this: all of you need to be very careful. They have been as close as the parking lot here. We know that. You know that. Mike took the brunt of it that night."

Branigan spoke up, his eyes searching the faces of his friends. "They'll be getting desperate, won't they? Trying to get to her. But why?"

"Cadee has something they want. We have some thoughts on that but we need to confirm that. Cadee, I want to go over any paperwork or files you brought back. Confidentiality is important, but we need to keep you alive. The rumour is that they want you dead, that you have something they need back.”

Cadee blanched, her hands tightening on Benen’s. “Why Benen?”

“To get to you. Plain and simple. Who can stay as close to you as he does? And he is the one who took you away from down there. Part of it is revenge or vengeance. Part of it is a terror or fear campaign to make you flee from where you are safe.”

Chapter 45

Benen walked quickly across the parking lot towards the building in the late morning the next day, his thoughts not on his surroundings but on Cadee. He felt sudden fear for her and quickened his steps to an almost run. He slid to a stop as a man appeared in front of him, a revolver pointed at him. His briefcase dropped from his hand as he raised both of them at a motion from the weapon. He sighed. What Will had feared had come to pass. Lord, please? Have Cadee somewhere she's safe. I can't lose her. I love her too much.

He was shoved into the building and then down to an empty office, stumbling at the violent shove he received that sent him through the door, barely able to keep to his feet. He spun, his eyes on the man, whose face was covered with a ski mask, before he backed away, hands once more in the air. His back hit the wall and he stood, almost afraid to breathe at the evil and violent that came from the man. Hearing a sound he glanced sideways, his heart falling as he saw his five team members there.

Benen's only thought was Cadee, praying she was safe, that someone had been able to get her to safety. Their captor backed away, the door closing behind him. The six men waited, not sure if they could move.

"Benen?" Branigan's voice was low. "Did you see Cadee?"

Benen's head dropped. "No. I was on my way there when he stopped me in the parking lot. The rest?"

"We don't know. We were each taken one at a time and brought here. That has happened over the last hour. Bradon sent Kade to Cadee, but I'm not sure she'll let him in with her." Branigan moved away from the wall, searching the room. "They'll have cameras or microphones in here. Guaranteed."

Brady pointed at the wall that contained the door. The other five men nodded and continued their search, finding the items Branigan had named. They spun as they heard the door open and stared as Cadee was shoved into the room, spinning in anger as she did so, her voice harsh as she told the men off in another language.

Benen froze, waiting for what he didn't know. He reached for Cadee, pulling her back, his arms holding her close to him, his eyes on the men who had followed her through the door. He couldn't see their masked faces, but the glittering cold angry eyes told the story. They were not likely to walk out of here, any of them, unless God intervened. He could hear the sharp breaths of the men around him.

The apparent leader approached, his eyes on Cadee, before he pulled her from Benen's arm and shoved her into a chair one of the men had placed in the centre of the room. He then turned to the six men, ordering them to the floor, to place their hands behind their necks, and to not move. The men exchanged glances before they heard a whimper from Cadee and saw the first man standing beside her, his weapon against her temple.

Benen dropped to the floor, keeping his eyes on his bride, praying harder than he had ever prayed before, begging, pleading that Cadee would survive. He didn't care about himself. He just wanted his bride and his friends to live.

He listened to the words, not understanding what the man saying, his gaze on Cadee, watching as she shook her head. Her eyes sought his, a plea for understanding in them, signalling her love to him.

She spoke to him, her voice calm, belying the fear he knew she felt. "It's okay, Benen. He doesn't want you men at all. I don't know what he wants. He's asking for a photo or a file. I don't have that. We went through everything. I have nothing that he describes."

Benen gathered himself to rise as the man struck Cadee across the face, before he was slammed back to the floor, pain ricocheting through him as he hit hard and then a booted foot has stamped on his neck, holding him still. He heard sounds from his friends and then a voice commanding silence. They all froze. Benen was not able to watch Cadee any more, not from the angle his head was at.

Cadee yelled at the man to let Benen go, to let him alone. She suffered another slap to the face, her hand rising to cup her cheek, her tongue finding the cut on her lip and the coppery taste of the blood. She blinked back tears as she glared at the man.

"Let him alone! He's done nothing!"

"On the contrary, my dear, he has. He brought you back here. He has kept you from me. You have something I want and you will give it to me." The man stood, arms folded, legs shoulder width apart, his eyes narrowed through the slits in the mask as he stared at her, anger in him.

"I don't have what you want. In fact, I have no idea what you want. You need to give me more details." Cadee prayed that the wire Will had worked up for her was working.

Will had approached her earlier that day, startling her with his request.

"A wire? Why?" She had stared at him and then Barnabas and Breck as they stood beside her.

"Because we have word they'll make an attempt today to get to you. If they do, a wire will help us to track you and we can listen in on what is being said." Will held up the tiny transmitter he had for her. "Only you can trigger it on. It will fit behind your watch, or in your shoe. Wherever you want to wear it."

She stared at it for the longest time, biting at her lips, her arms folded across her body, before she looked up at Barnabas and then Breck. Both men nodded at her.

"We need to, Cadee. We don't want to invade your privacy, but we need to ensure we can track you." Breck felt like he was pleading with her.

"But it's not just about me, is it, Barnabas?" Her question startled the men, Will turning to Barnabas, a frown on his face.

"What's she talking about, Barnabas?"

Barnabas shrugged, his eyes still on Cadee. "I have no idea. Cadee? Care to explain?"

"I'm sorry, Barnabas. I don't know why I said that. It's just I get hunches like this sometimes that are usually correct. It's like God uses me to warn someone. I dislike that so much and have told Him so. I've asked that He not do it any more, but He still does."

The three men had shared a look. They had heard of God working this way, but had never met someone He used.

"Cadee, do you know for sure what you are saying? Do you have any information or leads at all?" Will's voice was soft as he spoke, hushed by the presence of God.

She shook her head. "No, I'm sorry." Her eyes pled with them to understand. "I don't, not at the beginning. I just get impressions. But I can see evil approaching Barnabas. What shape or form, I'm not told. I may be told. I may not. Usually all I can do is say something to the person. It's up to them from there."

"And this has happened a number of times?" Breck spoke, his eyes on her before he looked at Barnabas, a frown on his face as he watched his friend and employer.

"It has. More frequently over the last two or three years. At times, I hate it." She turned away, rubbing at her eyes, before she turned back, her hand held out to Will. "Let me have that. I trust you." She slipped out of her runner, attaching the transmitter and then slipping her foot back into the shoe. "Will this really work?"

"It should, Cadee. As long as you don't lose your shoe. And it is waterproof."

She shrugged. "Then you'll be able to hear me the next time I'm dragged into the lake."

"Cadee!" Barnabas' voice had a note of shock as well as reproof.

"And you can't tell me something like that won't happen again, can you?" She stared down the men, who acknowledged she was right.

Chapter 46

Benen had no idea that Will had approached Cadee. He had been away since early in the morning, a client needing in-house help on an IT problem. He had been headed home when he was taken captive. He had no idea how the others had been taken. His heart raised in desperate pleas. He knew his friends were praying.

He felt the foot lift from his neck. He waited for it to return before he moved his head enough to watch Cadee. She was staring at him, a slight frown on her face before she looked down at her foot and then back at him. He frowned himself, wondering what she was trying to say.

Branigan's voice was low when he spoke. "Will's given her something."

"What?" Benen's voice was barely audible.

"Will was working on transmitters for you two. He has likely given her one."

"Silence!" The leader's voice rang through the room. Benen and Branigan both felt his wrath in the blows they took, pain searing through their bodies. Benen heard Cadee's voice but couldn't make out the words, only heard the rage in it as she yelled at the men. Cadee, he thought, this isn't helping. Please, Lord, get us out of here.

Cadee watched in horror at the abuse Benen and Branigan took, before she glared at the leader, who

———

210

watched her closely, his eyes still narrowed, the evil and anger she felt from him showing in them.

"You need to cooperate with us. Otherwise, these men will be hurt. And when we're done with them, we have eight others we will use." His words were harsh and brutal.

Benen tilted his head as he listened. He knew that voice, just could not place where he knew him from. His eyes found Brody who nodded. Brody knew him as well. Benen watched as Brody shot a look at the leader and then back to him, mouthing a name. Bene's heart sank. Brody was right. Now, how did they survive and bring this monster to justice?

The man left after a while, leaving two men in the room as guards. Cadee watched them closely, waiting for a chance to move. She knew she had the transmitter working. She had activated as she was grabbed, pretending she was losing her shoe, before she was roughly dragged through the building, first to Benen's office, which they had broken into, and then here. She had been captive for at least two hours, she thought, not taking a chance to glance at her watch to be sure. Her gaze shifted to the men where they lay on the floor, a frown on her face as she watched them. Cadee just knew that they were plotting something. She knew them well enough to know they weren't just laying there. Their minds were working on how to get them all free.

Barnabas stood behind the police barricade, at Will's side, his eyes on his building. He knew seven of the men were fine. They were lined up behind him, shoulder to shoulder, their eyes on the building as well.

"Will?"

Will shook his head. "Her transmitter is working. Smart lady to get that done. She's with the men now." He looked around, towards the command centre. "We'll get word if we have to move in."

"How many?" Breck's voice spoke up as he moved to stand beside Will.

"As far as we can tell, there are four plus the leader. Cadee's been feeding us information as she can, usually contained in her sentences to the leader." He paused, shaking his head. "She's good. We need her on our force."

"That will never happen." Buckley spoke up. "We've talked. She's not sure what she wants to do but it isn't that. She's afraid of police work. She saw too much down there. Cadee knows it's not the same but she told me the bad taste lingers."

Will excused himself as he heard his name called and walked towards the tech, spending a few moments in deep conversation as he studied the pages he had been handed. He shook his head as he turned to watch the building.

Barnabas had turned to watch him before he walked towards him.

"Will?"

"It's who we thought, Barnabas. Lance Logan. We have a rap sheet on him. He's brutal." He looked up at Barnabas. "We need to get in there and get them out. Any way in from the outside other than the door."

"There are windows, but it's a small office. If there are men in there, we wouldn't get in and out without them being aware of it."

Will nodded, his mind racing. "There's no one else in the building?"

Breck shook his head. "No. They were all away for the day. Amy was in Barnabas' office and we got to her and got her out."

"Good. I have my people moving in." Will stepped away as an officer ran towards him, before Will headed back that way with him.

Barnabas turned to his men. "We have to wait, guys. We have to let them do their job."

"I know we do, but what room are they in?" Burney spoke up.

"The one at the end, on the right, near the back entrance." Barnabas' voice slowed. "Come on, guys. We need to find Will. I had forgotten for a moment."

Chapter 47

Will stared at Barnabas, not quite sure he had heard correctly. "What are you saying?"

"There's a tunnel. We put it in years ago, because we needed to have a way out if there was trouble. I had forgotten it. Until Burney asked." Barnabas ran his hands through his hair. "How could I forget?"

"We've never used it, but I know it's inspected regularly." Breck stood with his back to the building and pointed carefully. "It comes out near that pile of rocks. They were put there to hide the entrance."

"Okay. We'll look into it. Which one of you comes with me?"

Breck stepped forward. "I'll go. I'm usually the one who is in on the inspections." He turned to Barnabas. "They'll be watching us, Barnabas. How do we hide the fact that Will and I are gone?"

Brennen spoke up. "Head back to the Command Centre and then for your car, Will. Breck goes with you. They'll think you're leaving. Breck can show you where to park so that you and some officers can head in through the woods. I doubt they'd be looking too hard that way."

Will and Breck headed away from the other men. Barnabas stood for a moment, undecided as to what to do, before he turned to the six remaining men.

"We can't just sit by. What can we do?"

"Come with me. Head off to the gym. We'll meet in there." Barnabas glanced around. "No one's watching us." His phone came out as he felt it vibrate. "Now, how did he manage that?"

"Who?" Buckley spoke for them all.

"Brady. He's gotten a text message off to me. There are two men in the room with them. Two other men beside the leader. They've left. Benen and Branigan have been beaten. He says Cadee's been hit, blood on her mouth."

"That's not good. We don't have much time, then, do we?" Brandon moved quickly towards the rear of the building, heading for the office there. "What do we need to do?"

"First, Buckley? Prayer." Barnabas stood beside him as the men circled, arms linking, as they prayed.

"Buckley, where are the packs?" Barnabas looked up as they finished.

"Here." Buckley reached for them. "I'm not sure we'll be able to get in, though. Will has his people all around."

"That's true, but there is one way." Barnabas spun in a circle before he headed for the gym again, for the wall facing the lake. "Here. Breck told them of one tunnel, but not this one. This one leads to Benen's office, right?"

"It does." Brandon shouldered his pack, the contents of which no one but the men knew. "I'll lead."

They quickly moved through the tunnel, Brennen in the rear, closing the door behind them. They stopped Brandon reached for the lock on the door, carefully opening it, before stepping through, the other six men behind them.

"Now what? Barnabas?" His voice low, Brody spoke for them all.

"We see where they are." Barnabas stood by the door, the door opened slightly. "I don't hear anyone in the hallway." He reached for the stick with the small camera on it that Brenden had pulled from his pack. "Let's see what they're up to."

They watched intently in the small screen of the tablet that showed the camera view.

"They're not out there. Where are they?"

"Lobby?"

Barnabas pulled the stick back quickly and shut the door, motioning for the men to flatten themselves along the wall, a finger to his lips as he set the stick and camera down behind him. They heard the footsteps and then the door knob turned, the door opening and a man entering. Brody had him on the floor, a hand over his mouth, before he could react. Hands quickly bound him and gagged him, and then carried him into Benen's office, the door closing to shut him in.

Chapter 48

Cadee watched through her lashes as the leader entered again. She had finally placed him, knew his name, but just didn't know why he wanted something from her. She had nothing but her own belongings. She was sure that was true for her parents as well.

She simply kept shaking her head as his questions, not seeing the looks of concern on the men's faces. They all knew she couldn't keep refusing to answer, that they would all pay for that if she did.

Cadee sought to find Benen, tears of pain blinding her eyes for a moment before she blinked them away. This man was getting more and more brutal. How could she stop him? She knew of no way. Benen was watching her, his face grim and sober, sorrow and concern for her in his eyes. He gave a subtle shake of his head, his eyes roaming the room before coming back to rest on her. She looked at the other men, frowning slightly as she saw their inattention to the men and their attention of the wall across from her.

She watched the leader as he left the room, taking one of the men with him, before she saw Branigan rise as the remaining man walked in front of the men. He had him down and unconscious from a blow to his chin before she could react. She drew in a deep breath, went to rise and then slumped back as the door reopened and the man entered, the other man with him.

The two men stopped, weapons drawn, as they stared around, not seeing their partner.

"Where is he?" The leader's voice was loud as he almost shouted the words. "Where is my man?"

Cadee's mouth was open to reply when a sound from behind him drew her attention. She screamed, drawing his eyes to her. His weapon raised even as Benen threw himself towards him. A scream broke from Cadee at the same time that a shot rang out. Benen's hand went to his head even as his body hit the floor, blood streaming from the crease mark left by the bullet, that traced along the side of his head. He didn't move after he went down, leaving Cadee staring at him in horror before she looked at the man.

"Why?"

"Because he was interfering with my plans for you." The man reached for her, pulling her to her feet.

She fought him, her hands and feet flying before she escaped and backed away, the five friends of Benen's on their feet, ready to attack when an opportunity arose.

He stared at her, before turning back to stare behind him, hearing a sound and then seeing the wall opening towards him, Will and four officers emerging, their own weapons drawn and pointed at the man.

"Put it down, Logan. Put your weapon down." Will's voice was hoarse with his emotions.

The man, known as Lance Logan, refused, his weapon still pointing at Cadee.

"Not a chance. She's my ticket out of here."

"You're not going anywhere. Your men outside? They're under arrest. It's just you and this one man now. You shoot, we shoot."

Their words volleyed back and forth, the eyes of everyone watching them. Cadee's eyes were on Benen, not sure if he was alive or dead. Her eyes flew to Logan as she heard him yelling, seeing the weapon pointing directly after her, before he fired. The shot hit her in the chest, sending her flying backwards to land on the floor with a thud.

Brady was running towards her, on his knees, his hands reaching to try and stem the flow of blood even as commotion erupted around them. He ignored the shouts and struggle, not daring to look around. Baird's hands were there to help him, Blair and Bradon working on Benen, Branigan standing with Will, watching as the men worked.

Will watched as Logan and his men were led away, Logan loudly demanding medical attention and crying police brutality. He shook his head before he turned back to the room, moving aside as paramedics were rushed in. Barnabas appeared at his shoulder, the other men standing in the hallway staring in, concern on their faces.

"Will?"

Will turned slightly, a frown on his face. "I have no idea how you got in, Barnabas, but we will talk about that. I hear you captured one of the men."

"No, two. They're in Benen's office." He looked past him at Breck. "We used the tunnel to Benen's office. You came in the one you needed to."

"You shouldn't have."

Barnabas shrugged. "We took a chance, Will. Now, what about Benen and Cadee?"

"Benen took a bullet along the side of the head. They're moving out with him now." Will moved them back so the stretcher bearing Benen could move past them. Benen was still unconscious, his face covered in blood, a large white bandage wound around his head.

"Cadee took a bullet to the chest. Brady was there right away, but I've called in an air ambulance." Will strode from the room, Barnabas at his side. "We need to clear this place, Barnabas. Get your men out."

Barnabas motioned to Burney's group, pointing to the door. "Come on, fellows. We need to clear out of here. We'll give our statements at some point. Right now, Branigan's team is stuck here. I want you with Doc and Anna, Ted and Mary, Berneen and Darby. I know they were kept away and kept safe. But now we need to meet at the hospital. Breck? I need to be here. Can you talk to them?"

Breck nodded. "I was going to suggest that. Come on, guys. Let's hit the road."

Barnabas watched the men as they walked away before he turned back to stare through the door at the men and women milling around, knowing that Brady was still in there, his hands helping to save Cadee. Or at least, that was his prayer. He knew she was hit

hard and bad just by the look on Will's face and on
the faces of the four of his men stalking in anger and
worry from the room.

Chapter 49

A hour later, Barnabas stood at Benen's bedside in the Emergency Department, his eyes on his friend, listening as the physician spoke.

"He'll have a headache when he awakens. No fractures. I don't see that any damage has been done to the eyes."

"That's a relief and an answer to prayer. Thanks, Doc." Barnabas reached to shake the physician's hand. "You said you were moving him to a floor?"

"We are. I understand a private room?"

"That's correct. A private room." Barnabas sighed. "When he awakens, we'll have to tell him about his wife."

"His wife? What about her?" The physician turned from where he had been headed for the door.

"His wife. Cadee. The gunshot to the chest." Barnabas had turned to the physician. "She was shot just after he was."

"That's his wife? I'm sorry. I didn't know that. I hadn't heard her name, only her condition." He sighed, returning to stare down at Benen. "Then, he's her next of kin."

"If you need authorization for treatment, her parents are in the waiting room, or in a conference room on this floor. I think that's where Will has them."

The physician nodded. "Someone else is treating her. I'll let them know." He looked down at Benen. "It will likely be a while before he awakens. If you need to have someone with him until he does, that can be arranged."

"Thank you. I know my friends would like that."

Barnabas finally headed for the conference room, his hand on the door before he opened it, a prayer raising for the people inside, for the two he had left behind him. He had no idea how bad Cadee had been hurt.

All eyes turned to him as he entered and then Ted and Mary were in front of him.

"Any word on Cadee?" Ted's voice held hope.

"Not that I know of, Ted. I did let them know you two were here. They'll be speaking with you shortly, I suspect."

"Benen?" Berneen spoke from his side, Baird's arm tight around her. It had been too close once more for them.

"He's still out. But other than a headache, the doctor doesn't expect any lasting damage."

"But Cadee? How is she?" Baird spoke, knowing what he had seen.

"I haven't been told yet." Barnabas turned as the door opened and Brady entered, wearing a pair of hospital scrubs.

"Brady?" All eyes were on him as Mary spoke.

"Mary, Ted. They asked me to find you. They need to talk to you about Cadee." His voice was calm, but the ones who knew him best read in his eyes his emotions and prayers began to flow.

"She's alive?"

Brady nodded. "She is, but barely. They're wanting to take her to surgery, but they need signatures for that. Benen can't, but you're listed as next of kin after him."

He watched as they walked away from him before he motioned for Barnabas to follow him.

The two men stood back from where Ted and Mary had been met by the physician, Ted's arm going around Mary as she collapsed against him.

"Brady? What couldn't you say?" Barnabas turned to him, his eyes watchful, his heart praying.

"She may not make it through surgery, Barnabas. It's close to the heart. They aren't sure if they can even remove the bullet."

"So, Logan may win after all."

Brady shook his head. "No. Will was through. Logan tried to run, grabbed an officer's gun."

"And they shot him." Barnabas' hands clenched. "He's dead?"

Brady nodded. "He is. Will regrets that. They will be questioning the men with him but they don't think the men know much. He thinks there's someone else out there. Someone who hired Logan."

"He's the hit man?"

Brady nodded, even as he turned at footsteps behind him and saw the men encircling them. "Logan was the hit men. The others were ones he hired. I would say they not likely knew exactly what he was up to."

Buckley spoke up. "We have the prayer chain at church going. Jace has seen to that." He stopped speaking, his face whitening. "It has to be someone from the church. But who?"

Barnabas' hand stopped on his face as he heard the words. "Of course. It has to be. We need to talk to Will."

"And here he comes." Breck moved aside for Will to enter their group.

"Barnabas? Word on Benen and Cadee?" He was worried, he had seen the looks on the faces of the paramedics as they had rushed Cadee to the air ambulance and knew just how close it was for her.

"Benen's moving to a room soon. I gather you have men waiting for that?" Barnabas watched Will nod. "Cadee's headed for surgery." He turned as he heard wheels on the floor and the me stepped aside, their faces tightened in anger as they watched Cadee move past them, Ted and Mary following. Doc and Anna appeared in the doorway of the conference room, Berneen and Darby with them, before they walked to Cadee's parents and arms around them, walked with them to the elevator. No words were necessary.

Chapter 50

Two days later, Benen sank into a chair beside Cadee's bed, his eyes first on all the equipment that surrounded her, before he reached for her hand, feeling the limpness of it. This was not how he expected to spending two days before Christmas, sitting in a hospital ICU room, not knowing if his bride would live or die. He reached to touch her face, what he could see of it, speaking words to her that he could not remember speaking. When a nurse touched his shoulder and told him he needed to leave, he shook his head and then nodded, rising to kiss his wife and then walk slowly from the room, grief weighing him down.

His five team members were waiting for him as he approached, ready to sit with him, to pray with him and for him. He nodded at their words, sinking down into a chair, his head pounding. He had been warned but didn't care. The only one that mattered was in the room down the hall. Cadee's surgeon had spoken at great length with him and her parents, indicating just how serious it was for her, how close it had been. He had finally sent Ted and Mary home for a break, telling them they would be needed when she awoke, and awake she would, he was adamant on that.

Two days later, Christmas morning dawned bright and sunny. Benen stood once more in the ICU room, his eyes on Cadee's face, his hand on hers, the other hand around her shoulders as his tears wet her hair. The ventilator had been removed the night before, but she still had not awakened. That concerned her surgeon. He had stated that she should have.

His thoughts turned to prayer. Benen knew they were both bathed in prayers of many, but he still felt so alone, as if there wasn't anyone but him. He knew God had protected them, even when he hadn't been able to protect her.

He felt Cadee moving, something she had not done yet, and he straightened up, his eyes on her face as she blinked, opening her eyes and then closing them again.

"I hurt." Her voice was rough and hoarse.

Benen grinned slightly. That was his Cadee, he thought. Honest to a point.

"Cadee, my darling, you're awake."

Her eyes opened and she stared at him for a moment. "Benen? What are you doing here? What time is it?" Then, she groaned. "Logan. Where is he?"

"He won't bother you again, my darling. He's gone to face a higher judge than one on earth. And it's Christmas morning."

"Christmas morning? We have the dinner in a few hours. I need to help." She tried to push back the blankets and found she had no strength to do that.

"Cadee, you can't. You had surgery five days ago. You're still in ICU." Benen's hands reached for hers. "You have to lie still."

She stared up at him, a frown on her face. "You were shot."

"Just a crease that knocked me out. Not like you."

"Why? What happened to me? And why am I in ICU?" She looked around, her head twisting to stare at the various pieces of equipment before she touched the IV line running to her hand.

"I almost lost you. You were shot. The bullet was close to the heart but they were able to get it out. The surgeon stated he shouldn't have but he felt other hands on his. I told him that was God. He stared at me and then nodded."

"That is what God does. I have seen it before. Now I have experienced it." She yawned, her eyes sliding closed as she slipped away into a natural sleep just as the nurse entered the room.

A week later, she was home, pampered to the point she was frowning at Benen every time he approached her. She was tired of being in bed and told him that. He had stood before he reached to wrap her in a blanket and carry her through to his office, making a place for her on the couch before he tucked blankets around her.

"Thank you, love." She snuggled down, her eyes on him as he sat behind his desk. "I didn't really mean to grumble."

"I know you didn't. You're not used to being still. Just rest." Benen's attention went to his work, not on her, missing her watching him.

Two hours later, he rose and stretched, standing watching her sleep, before he padded on socked feet through to the kitchen, pausing as he heard a tap at the door. Opening it, he stepped aside for Barnabas and Breck to enter.

"Coffee?" At their nod, Benen poured three mugs of coffee and pointed to the living room. "Cadee's asleep in the office. What can I do for you?"

"We need to talk to you both. It's important enough that I think you should wake her." Barnabas looked up at a sound and then rose. "Cadee?"

Benen was on his feet, reaching for her. "Cadee?"

She looked distressed. "I know who it was, Benen. I know who hired Logan." She hid her face against her husband. "It was Jace's brother. John."

"That's correct, Cadee. Will arrested him this morning. He has confessed. He had a grudge against your father for some slight in the years past. What it was? He was in love with your mother but she chose your father instead. He had never forgiven him that. He didn't tell Logan that was why he was after you, for revenge, but told him that you had something of his that he wanted back."

"All this over that? He almost killed me. Hurt Benen. How many others did he destroy?" Cadee's voice was sad.

"We'll never know. With the mission closed, all those that could have been reached haven't been." Barnabas grew silent, sorrow for that in his heart.

"Your Dad's reopening it, isn't he, Barnabas?" Benen's voice was quiet, but assured.

"He is. How did you know?" Barnabas stared at him.

"He talked to us, got our thoughts on that. Ted and Mary's as well. He wants to use them in the office, with their experience. Cadee has been offered a position there as well."

Breck spoke. "But she won't." He simply grinned as she frowned at him.

"And why not?"

"Because you can't keep track of us all if you're not around here. You do that well, Cadee." Breck looked at Benen, his head tilted as he studied the other man. "Do you know what your wife did for Christmas?"

"No, I don't. I didn't think she could do anything for Christmas, being in ICU at the time." His arm tightened around her as he gazed down at her.

"Each one of the men received a gift bag from her. In it was a CD of their favourite artist, autographed at that. One of your photos with their favourite verse on it, framed. A devotional book that she knew we all wanted. That's what your wife has done. She looks at a person, delves deep and finds what each one needs to be encouraged. Not many people have that gift. She needs to be used by God for that."

Cadee had stilled as Breck had begun to speak, knowing what he was going to tell. "I had to, Breck.

I couldn't not do that. You all welcomed me into the family here, not knowing me. Welcomed me first for God's sake, then for Benen. Then we became friends and I felt your welcome for me. You took in my parents. You have shown Christ's love in that. You put your lives on the line for me. How could I not do what God prompted?"

Barnabas had to clear his throat before he spoke. "That's the embodiment of Barnabas in the Bible, Cadee. You have put hands and feet to what Dad and I envisioned with The Foundation. I think we need to bring you on staff."

She shook her head, her eyes huge. "I couldn't do that. I couldn't work for a company that has that much money behind it."

The men laughed even as Barnabas assured her she was just the person they had been looking for and hadn't known it. They would talk in the new year, he said.

Cadee watched as Benen walked back towards her, before he sat on the couch and just wrapped her in his arms, his voice praying for them both, before he grew silent and just held her.

A month later, Benen leaned against Cadee's desk in her office down the hall from his, watching with amusement as Barnabas and Cadee argued amicably about her duties. She was adamant she was the wrong person, but Benen knew she was where God wanted her. They had talked many times about it.

Cadee finally turned to Benen when they were alone, walking into his arms, her own around him. She still struggled with weakness and fatigue, but had been told that was to be expected, given what she had been through. She sighed, thankful that God had protected them, kept them safe, kept them alive. The court cases were upcoming, but she had no fear of facing her enemies. God had spoken to her, helped her to forgive them and move on. She knew Benen struggled at times, not sure how to forgive but he assured her he was working on that, him and God.

Benen tilted his head to look down at her. "Still not sure?"

"I'm not but everyone else seems to be. I just need time, Benen. I've been through so much, and this is something I have thought about for years, but never thought I would have an opportunity to serve God in this way. Mom and Dad are happy where they are. Did you know they are planning to move into a bungalow near the mission office?"

"I knew that. Your Dad and I talked. They feel that's where they need to be." He looked down at her, all his love for her in his eyes and on his face. "I never dreamed all those years ago, when we were such good friends in college, that you would be mine for life. I love you, Cadee Rose."

"And I love you, Benen. It's not fair." Her voice grew grumpy.

"What's not fair?" He was puzzled.

"I have two names. You only have one. What were your parents thinking?"

He shouted with laughter. "It's tradition that the males only have one name in my family. Just the way it works." He grinned at the face she pulled. "Are you telling me that any sons we have will have two names?"

"You'd better believe that." She looked up at him. "Thank you, Benen, for being my protector. I know at times it was hard and there were those incidents where you couldn't, but you tried."

"I know, my darling. I know. God was gracious. Now, we need to go out to lunch to celebrate?" He turned her towards the door, reaching for their coats, turning out the lights to the freshly painted and decorated office in the colours and theme that Cadee loved.

"Celebrate?" She slipped into the coat he held for her before he reached for her hand.

"Celebrate. Yes, we need to celebrate. Your new job. Our marriage, which we haven't had a chance to celebrate yet. That I have the love of my life with me. Too many things to enumerate.”

She laughed, a carefree one that echoed through the lobby of the building as they headed for the outside doors. “Only you, Benen, could put it that way. And I have the love of my life with me as well.”

Dear Readers

Thank you for choosing to pick up the story of Benen and his lady love, Cadee. What a wild ride they took me on as an author! Not what I had planned, but God gave the words to me, moved my fingers to work.

Evil is all around us. As Christians, we can sometimes sense it stronger at times than at others. I have had this happen to me. At those times, that is when I feel the protection God provides surrounding me, bringing me through. We will never know on earth just what or who God had protected us from.

God bless each one of you.

Ronna